# WHERE DID SHE GO?

## A MICHELLE WATSON THRILLER

## ALEC PECHE

*I would like to thank my first reader GM and my editor Ellen Falk for cleaning up my problems with spelling and grammar.*

*In every book I learn something new. Besides my intensive research on modern day Venezuela, I also learned that Colombia the country is spelled differently than my alma mater Columbia University. Both are probably shuddering at my stupidity for admitting this blank in my knowledge. I likely learned this in grade school, but sadly my brain deleted that fact to make room for the stories in my head.*

*Cheers,*
*Alec*

# CHAPTER 1

$\mathcal{M}$ ichelle Watson, CIA Case Officer, had a little more than twenty-four hours to be briefed on her next assignment and visit her adult children. Her condominium was in Virginia, and she had a second home in San Martin, California, which was near her kids. She would achieve both objectives despite the distance and the fat folder in front of her. She texted her kids to say that she had arranged a six-hour stopover in San Jose so she could check on her property and them.

"How about dinner at my house?" Ashley, her daughter, replied.

"Sarah and I will see you at Ashley's," her son Tyler, responded. "Do you need a ride from the airport?"

"No, I already arranged a rental car as I want to check on my house and it will be such a short layover. Great! See you soon. Love you, M."

Michelle looked at her watch and planned to spend a few hours going through the file before teleporting to her home. She opened the file and began to read about the sale of arms to Venezuela by Iran. Both countries disliked the US and suffered sanctions by the US that affected their economies. That made them bedfellows in their attitudes. More importantly, Iran had weapons; and Venezuela was geographically closer to the US, some of Iran's weapons would be able to reach US shores if launched from Caracas.

As a former policewoman, Michelle was used to looking at the means and motive behind criminal actions. Those same principles worked for understanding the evil people that she was trying to take down for the CIA. Both countries had motives, and when they combined geography and weapons, they had means. Okay, that was the root of this mission—determine if the wrong kind of arms were arriving in Venezuela and decipher what both countries' intentions were. It was quite an assignment for her and her partner, Jason Smith. Of course, they were backed up by the analysts at the agency, but she and Jason were the boots on the ground, sourcing out new intelligence.

Jason had departed on a commercial jet for Curaçao. He would be landing this evening and then renting a sailboat for the two of them to sail to Caracas. The amount of time she spent aboard the sailboat with him depended on two issues: did the boat make her seasick, and did she need to teleport somewhere to gather information. She had a history of seasickness, but she hadn't been on a sailboat in the Caribbean, so only time would tell. If she was seasick, then she would teleport back and forth between a hotel room somewhere in that region and his boat. She could just as easily teleport home, but it was good to stay in the region as the weather was similar. Going from a cold Virginia spring to the muggy Caribbean several times a day would likely lead her into a sinus infection.

She finished her first pass of the file and decided to head out to California. She had people who took care of her property, but it was always good to reconnect with her community, who unlike her children, were aware of her special talent. Given that the entire town had some sort of special talent, she could relax her guard around the residents of San Martin. Most of her friends had talents related to their occupations–special baked goods, amazing wineries, and even auto mechanics in San Martin who could magically fix cars. Michelle's talent hadn't shown itself until she nearly died after being shot during a routine traffic stop. Being able to magically move around the world sounded like great fun, and it was, except she couldn't take anyone with her. In fact, she couldn't take anything at all that wasn't in a backpack or the pockets of her garments. After she burned through the thrill of travel, she knew she needed to find a day job that brought meaning to her life, protected her loved ones, and made the world a better place. She also worried that if the world learned of her special abilities, she would be on everyone's hit list as she was a devastatingly good spy.

She arrived inside her California house closet. Even if there were thieves in her house, they wouldn't catch her arrival. Fortunately, the coast was clear, and she took a moment to examine if all was right with her property. She had a gardener who managed her small vineyard. She sold her grapes to another winery in town. Everything looked good; the house was spotless, and the plants were thriving. She backed her car out of the driveway, intending to head to her small town's main street. She was in the mood for some magical bakery items. In fact, she planned to take a large package of cookies with her when she met Jason. It was always good to have magical cookies when working in a foreign, hostile land. Later she traded cars with one of the townspeople and set forth to her daughter's house. After saying she had a rental car, it wouldn't do to arrive in her own car.

She hadn't visited her kids in a few months, and there was nothing like catching up with their lives in person. They both worked for technology companies that dotted the landscape of Silicon Valley. Her daughter was twenty-three and just a year from making the transition from college to work. On the side, Ashley had been taking cooking classes and Michelle was interested to see what she would prepare for their meal. Her son, Tyler, was a little older and married now for just over a year and would bring his wife, Sarah. Both kids had healthy relationships with their father and his second wife. They were good kids, and she was proud of them, even if they didn't know of her secret teleportation talent. She'd brought it up as she was recovering from the gunshot wound, and they hadn't believed her and, in fact, were quite distressed over her mental well-being. While she was sure she could convince them of her special talent now, she would bring them new distress if they knew what her day job really involved.

She parked on the street near Ashley's apartment and was buzzed inside. She was soon hugging her daughter, then her son, and finally her daughter-in-law. Ashley had opted for pizza for dinner, while Tyler and Sarah brought Crème brûlée knowing it was his mother's favorite dessert.

"How are the cooking classes going? I thought you might prepare something special today not that pizza isn't special," Michelle added.

"We're only going to see you for a few hours, so it seemed a shame to spend those hours with me in the kitchen. Besides, didn't we do well with providing your favorite foods?" Ashley asked.

"You did indeed. I've been out of the office on assignment frequently and in some foreign countries that have odd definitions of the word *pizza*."

Tyler frowned and said, "I thought the CIA had you doing just desk work. Why are you being sent outside of the United States? You mentioned a stopover. Where did you arrive from?"

"I just came from Tahiti. They wanted me to do some real-time data collection with boots on the ground. I'm enjoying that much more than the straight desk work."

Now both of her children were frowning. Michelle realized they had her glued to a desk somewhere safe from the world's menaces. They were convinced in their minds that she was safe and working in a low-key job. If they only knew that she had recently saved the world from destruction. Some day she might tell them when the time was right.

"I've been to Cuba to assess how our open borders are going. I've been to Morocco to assess how the people feel about their king. It helps the State Department and the CIA create briefs on the various countries and their political structure. Stuff like that, but I'm not in harm's way. I don't carry a gun, and I hear more gunshots at home than I do in these countries. Also, what I've told you is confidential. Please don't share my travels with your friends."

Ashley thought about what her mother was saying and asked, "Can I give you a list of special ingredients I want from the various countries? If you happen to be assigned there, you can pick up the item for me. It will be small stuff like a small bottle of Madagascar vanilla."

"Sure, give me a list. I can't guarantee that I'll be in the right country for any items, but I'll see what I can find."

Ashley was still frowning, but then she spent a few minutes and made out a short list. Michelle took a moment to review the list vowing to get an item off her daughter's wish list when she was done with the case. She could easily teleport to Madagascar and purchase a bottle, place it in her backpack, and head home. It would take her longer to find the item in the market than it would to travel there and back. That was the beauty of her skill.

"What time does your plane leave? Do you have a non-stop flight home?" Tyler asked.

Michelle looked at her watch and replied, "I'll need to leave in about thirty minutes. I'm fortunate enough to catch a ride with another CIA team on a private plane. That gives me more time to spend with you guys as the security, boarding, and departure process takes a lot less time than a commercial jet. Why don't the three of you catch me up on your lives in our remaining time?"

"Cool," replied Tyler. "I mean cool about the private jet."

"Yeah, makes me happy as I can travel faster."

They moved on to talking about their lives, and before Michelle was ready to leave, her alarm went off on her phone, telling her it was time to move on. With hugs and kisses, she said goodbye to her children and took the car back to the friend she borrowed it from. Moments later she was inside her condominium in Maryland ready to continue reviewing the file on their next mission. She finished reading, then hit the gym for what was likely her last workout until the mission was complete. Just before she closed her eyes, she checked on Jason's flight, and it appeared that his plane would arrive on schedule. Michelle would arrive after he'd arranged the boat rental, as there was nothing for her to do as he navigated the flights, customs, baggage, and boat rental.

# CHAPTER 2

*J*ason Smith, a CIA case officer and sailor, arrived in Curaçao after a connection in Panama. In his travels for the CIA, he had visited the Caribbean before, but not this island. The closest he'd come was drinking the liqueur named after the island. The airport was a little bit of a drive from the largest city and its seaport where he hoped to rent a boat. In the interim, he was checking into a hotel as it would take him time to find the perfect boat to rent and stock it with supplies. There were five marinas and his request to rent a boat for up to a month was likely unusual.

He did his research before he left Virginia and rented a two-bedroom bungalow for four weeks. Michelle could occupy one of the rooms as much as she needed if she had to escape seasickness. The bungalow would be one of their bases until this mission was complete. He checked into the room and sent Michelle a picture so she could teleport to Curaçao. He had to admit, he was enjoying working with her. Her special skill of teleportation had come in handy in their last case as she saved them from both bullets and hypothermia with her ability to move. As far as Jason was concerned, Michelle was the best partner ever.

He was startled as she appeared in front of him. It sort of reminded him of the old TV show, "Star Trek." She could just beam herself somewhere and pursue some piece of fact-finding related to their case. Their previous case had her visiting over one-hundred locations looking for a building in which weapons-grade uranium was being enriched. Her ability to visit so many physical sites in a small amount of time had put his guard up. Was she cheating? Was she taking photos off the internet instead of actually visiting them? He couldn't stand not knowing how she was collecting information, so he'd picked the locks of her home and waited for her to come home. That was when he learned her secret and appreciated the unique skill she brought to the CIA. He told their supervisor and Michelle that he was glad she decided to work for the good guys. She could be rich and have everything in her power if she wanted to pursue the dark side of humanity. She also knew that if her skill became known around the world, she would rise to everyone's number one target to kill.

"Welcome to Curaçao."

"Thanks, let me unload my backpack. Which bedroom have you taken?" Michelle looked good in shorts and a t-shirt with a heavy backpack. She was a little above average in height and slender. Her brown hair was tucked up in a knot. She worked out regularly and it showed. She was a fit woman. Michelle was in her early fifties, much like Jason.

He pointed to the bedroom holding his gear. In actuality it didn't matter—both bedrooms had en-suite bathrooms and were exactly the same. He followed her to the door of her bedroom and leaned against the doorframe while she went to work emptying her backpack.

"Here is a bag of cookies. There are likely the best you've ever tasted, and they'll make you feel happy."

"Are they made with marijuana?" Jason asked, looking suspiciously at the bag.

"Absolutely not. Just enjoy them." Michelle had no intention of revealing that they were magical cookies.

Jason took a bite of the first cookie and closed his eyes in enjoyment. "These are fabulous, thanks."

"Did you enjoy the quick visit with your kids?"

"Yes. My daughter, Ashley, gave me a list of things to buy in foreign countries when I'm on assignment. When we're finished with this assignment, I'll drop into Madagascar and buy her some vanilla."

"Do you ever think about telling your children about your real job and your ability to teleport?"

"On occasion, I feel like telling them, but two things stop me. First, they would be hurt that I waited this long to tell them, and second, they think I have a boring analyst job at the CIA and I just do computer searches to supply real agents with necessary information. They don't have to worry about me getting hurt on the job. They nearly lost me when I was shot as a cop, and I don't want them to have to worry about that happening again."

Jason thought about her reasoning and understood her conclusion. He'd never had children himself, but he could imagine wanting to give your children a soothing picture of what you did for a living.

"I guess I would do the same thing in your shoes. Once you unpack, I'll give you a brief tour, so you'll have the lay of the island. Then I want to check at a few marinas for a boat rental. I looked before I left, but all I saw were day charters. I'm sure with the right amount of money, I can talk them into renting me a boat for four weeks."

"What happens if it gets damaged during our op? The CIA will pay for a replacement, right? I've never destroyed anything so I wouldn't know."

"Didn't you drive a snowmobile into a Russian truck?" Jason asked, amused.

"I did, but I think the agency borrowed the snowmobile. No one seemed distressed that I destroyed it."

"Well, over my long career, I've destroyed many things. Depending on where you are in the world, it may or may not be a problem. The boat we're going to rent will be in the category of an expensive item I shouldn't let get destroyed, so we need to avoid being torched or blown up."

"Got it. Likewise, we need to make sure we don't destroy this bungalow."

"I think you're such a critical asset for the CIA that you could have a multi-million dollar budget to pay for things you destroy each year."

"Let's not test that theory with our lives or anyone nearby," Michelle said straightening and tossing her backpack onto a chair. She was done unpacking. "Let's go."

At the third marina they visited, Jason spied a boat that would be perfect for this mission. It was big enough to be comfortable for a journey on the open sea, yet small enough that he could operate it by himself. An hour later, after his bona fides were checked and a significant deposit placed, the boat was theirs. They left to shop for the supplies they would need. In addition to food and drink, Jason wanted scuba gear, a rigid inflatable boat and motor, and an underwater sea scooter. While Michelle could easily get onto a boat, but he needed to get there the old-fashioned way. He also needed extra air tanks for the scuba gear and scooter. He planned to load the boat with food for a week at a time, knowing that he should be in various ports on at least a weekly basis. Also, Michelle could bring a duffle full of food if need be.

Next, they had a call with Sheila Meeks, their supervisor at the CIA. The agency was monitoring the movement of the ship.

"Enjoying the weather in Curaçao?" Meeks asked.

"We just got here and there's glorious sunshine and heat. While the heat feels good, I'm glad we have A/C at the hotel and aboard the boat. I'm also glad I'm staying in this temperate zone and not testing my sinuses by bouncing between Maryland and the Caribbean," Michelle said.

"We visited several marinas before we found the right boat to rent without a crew. Then we went shopping to stock the provisions. Tomorrow we'll sail to Bonaire, and then on the following day we should cross over to Venezuela," Jason said.

"Where's the warship?" Michelle asked.

"It just past the cape of Africa and is heading slowly up the west coast. The African continent is 1,600 miles from Brazil, so they will probably sail close to the coast and then cross at the narrowest point, then sail north around the tip of South America and west to Venezuela. It is actually not a single ship, rather it's three ships. We estimate the height of the missile will be between one hundred and one-hundred-ten feet. All three ships are long enough to contain something of that length."

"Is there rocket fuel aboard the ships? Don't you need special gas to fire a rocket?" Michelle asked.

"Have you been reading up on rockets?" Jason asked her.

"A little, but there is so much science—physics and chemistry involved that I can barely understand. Mostly I was looking at pictures so I could recognize a rocket when it was in front of me."

Sheila looked at Michelle and asked curiously, "So, can you recognize a rocket?"

"I can recognize the shape and size of a rocket. I can take a picture of any other odd thing I might see and ask for help identifying the object."

"Did we put that in your briefing packet?" Sheila asked.

"No. I looked at it on the internet. After my experience with uranium enrichment centrifuges, I like to have pictures of what I might be seeing. I also looked up the ship pictures, though you included that in the packet. I was curious about what random people might be posting about the ships."

"Did you find anything unique in the public pictures?" Jason asked.

"No."

"If they continue on the current path and speed, they should arrive in Venezuela in about seven or eight days. Assuming they don't stop anywhere along the way. Brazil and Iran are trading partners, so perhaps the ship will stop in a Brazilian port. You two will be in Caracas in three days, correct?"

Michelle looked at Jason as she had no clue as to the sailing time.

"Yes. Tomorrow we'll stop in Bonaire, and then we'll cross over to the South American Continent stopping in Puerto Cabello in northwest Venezuela to pick up any intelligence, then it's on to Caracas, or rather the port that services Caracas."

"I'll send you periodic updates on the position of the ships. As these are large ships, check the ports that handle ships of this size for gossip. See if you can find documentation of ship arrival times."

"Will do," Jason and Michelle said together, then they smiled at each other over their timing.

The call ended.

"Let's go find dinner. I checked the weather and I'd like to set sail around eight in the morning."

"That sounds like a plan. At least I'll know early if I can stand being on the boat in the open ocean."

"If any day on a boat is going to be pleasant for you on open water, it's tomorrow. Little wind is projected, which leads to smaller waves. No hurricanes in the forecast over the next two weeks."

"Gee whiz, I didn't even think of that issue. Do they strike this region very often?"

"Bonaire, Aruba, and Curaçao are outside of the hurricane belt and therefore only get hit by a hurricane every twenty-nine years or so. Venezuela will occasionally have heavy waves from a hurricane off-shore, but hurricane season hasn't started yet."

"And this isn't the 29th year?"

"No," Jason said smiling.

"At least I have a way to get off a boat that is making me sick if we do run into waves." Then she had another thought, "We're not going near the Bermuda triangle, are we?"

"No. The triangle represents the area from the tip of Bermuda to the tip of Florida to San Juan, Puerto Rico. We're hundreds of miles away from that location."

While they had been discussing the weather, they walked toward a restaurant that Jason wanted to try. They discontinued their discussion about their mission until after they were seated and left alone in a corner of the establishment.

"Have you ever been on a mission to Venezuela? It seems like it might be a CIA hotspot," Michelle asked.

"No, I don't speak Spanish fluently enough, nor with the right accent to be of any good to the agency. I'll be able to understand what people are saying, but the moment I open my mouth, the game is over. I have sailed in the Caribbean, but more in the area of Jamaica or Barbados. I was on vacation, not on a mission. So, this will be new."

"I'm pretty good at understanding Spanish, but I speak poorly half Spanglish with a little Charades thrown in."

"I've googled the marinas and roads around the port. When we get back to the hotel, let's go over that and plan where we want to place ourselves. I think we should pretend to be a married couple on a boat vacation, with a fascination with big ships. That will be our purpose for searching the harbor for the Iranian ships. I asked the analysts to send me pictures of a variety of ships as part of that cover. They're on my phone."

"Do you have a picture of the Iranian ship? I'm so tempted to just teleport to it, but I need a safe place to appear and a picture in my head of what it looks like. It's weird how this teleportation skill requires my mind to imagine a landing spot. I can't imagine GPS coordinates and end up somewhere. I guess it has to do with the exactness of location. Isn't GPS good for something like six feet, and my magic needs a more precise location."

"That is weird, but I'm just grateful you have the skill. The world as we know it might have ended last month if not for your skill. Certainly, I would likely be dead from hypothermia. So, I'm grateful for whatever magical mechanism allows you to move around planet Earth. I think our analysts are monitoring the ships via satellite and they should be able to tell us where it is safe to land on the ships without landing on top of someone. They probably have routine patrols."

"Lots to research tonight before we leave. Do you have a satellite connection for the boat? Will we be able to surf the web or use our phones?"

"We should have full internet capabilities onboard the boat. I've brought equipment for that, including a printer. However, I have to think that the hotel wi-fi will be faster, so yes, more research tonight."

They moved the conversation on to what they would be seeing on their upcoming boat trip. Michelle wished she'd had more time before this case. She would have liked to become scuba certified given where they were, but there was probably no time for pleasurable pursuits despite the feeling of being on a vacation. Regardless, she brought her facemask. She could have asked Jason to train her to use the underwater scooter he bought, but she had other ways of moving around quickly.

# CHAPTER 3

$\mathcal{A}$s planned, they departed the harbor early with a sheaf of printouts from their research late into the previous night. They cleared the harbor in Curaçao, and Jason directed the sailboat east toward Bonaire. So far, the sea was relatively calm, and Michelle was weathering the waves. She knew she wouldn't want to eat any meals aboard the boat, but it was about a seven-hour journey to the next island, and she would eat onshore once they reached their marina.

She was impressed with the weather, the boat, and Jason's prowess as a captain.

"It's so beautiful out here and relaxing. I think I might fall asleep."

"I've always enjoyed being out on a boat for that very reason. I find that I am at peace with the world and there are no criminals in my immediate vicinity. The warm weather makes it all the more relaxing. But don't fall asleep as you'll fry in the sun."

"Thanks, that's good advice."

Michelle looked around for a shady spot and was soon dozing.

Jason noticed that Michelle had fallen asleep, so with one eye on his radar and GPS, he relaxed into the beauty of the ocean and monotonously steering the boat and thought about how they would insert themselves into places of gossip. He thought their cover was good. At least in Bonaire, they would be on friendly ground. It was good to take the boat on a test run before heading into enemy waters. Hopefully, with the boat's registration to Curaçao, they could, despite their American accents, act like they were ex-pats living in that country.

Jason watched the radar for nearby ships. His research showed that they didn't have to worry about pirates until they got closer to Caracas. An hour later, Michelle woke up and approached him, "Do you need me to steer so you can take a nap?"

"Do you know how to steer?" Jason asked with his eyebrow raised dubiously.

"No, but you could show me; I'm a quick study."

He was tired and thought about the journey.

"Okay, follow the course laid out here," Jason said pointing to a computer tablet. "There's a route drawn on it and you just have to steer the boat to stay on top of that line. Literally, you spin the wheel left or right to make course corrections. Don't drive yourself nuts by trying to stay exactly on top of the line."

"Got it. Sweet dreams."

He disappeared below presumably to a bed while Michelle continued to steer. She used the time to write a script that they would use to talk to people. She thought back to her days as a policewoman before she'd been shot. She enjoyed interviewing suspects and was one of the best at her job. She liked to think that her expertise came from observing body language. Everyone had tells, and she was better than most in seeing them. Jason had been undercover many times for the CIA, but she hadn't. She would need Jason to slow down her approach to gaining information. He was more likely to have the ability to behave like someone in retirement leisurely going about the world. She on the other hand would want to pummel people with questions in a rush to find information. She knew little of the culture in this part of the world, but she suspected her usual approach wouldn't be well received.

Two hours later, she had the script worked out and was just waiting for Jason to reappear from his nap. She was somewhat surprised that he had left her alone for several hours given that this was her first time steering a boat. She had to admit, though, it was foolproof. It was so easy to stay on top of the line. She also discovered that she was a little less seasick. Perhaps much like driving a car, steering a boat gave the brain a little more anticipation of movement which kept her stomach settled.

She could see Bonaire in the distance and on the GPS screen. She thought she had perhaps another hour of steering before they reached the island. If Jason didn't wake up in the next half hour, she would have to leave the helm and wake him up. She had no idea about how to dock the boat. As the island got closer, Michelle kept checking her watch. She was relieved to see Jason appear looking refreshed.

"I was about to come and wake you up. I have no idea how to dock this boat."

"I set my alarm to wake me up about thirty minutes before we reached the harbor in Bonaire. You did a great job steering."

"It was pretty idiot-proof, which is why you probably got a good rest. I'll have to watch what you do in case I ever have to bring this boat into the harbor. Do you have the GPS set for a specific bay in a specific yacht club?"

"I do. I made a reservation before we left. We'll come into the bay as the engines power down at the harbor village marina. We'll tie the boat up and head for customs as we have to have our passports checked."

"Are you staying aboard the boat tonight?" Michelle asked.

"Why, aren't you?"

"Nope, I'm spending the night at our hotel in Curaçao. I won't sleep if the boat rocks or if I hear people nearby. So, are you staying here, or did you book a hotel?"

"I booked a hotel. This might be the last luxury shower I'll get for a few days. Fortunately, this boat has a small shower, so hopefully I won't stink."

"What time do we set sail in the morning?"

"Early. We're going to head south toward Puerto Cabello and continue sailing through the night and arrive the next day. We may begin to see pirates once we move into these Venezuelan waters."

"Pirates? Why didn't you mention that before? I still have time to go home and get weapons. What do we need?"

"I have the drone onboard the boat that I plan to launch to get a better look at any suspicious boats. If we are approached by pirates, they'll be in a faster boat and have automatic weapons. We don't want to get into a gun battle with them."

"I could always land on their boat and pull the pin on a grenade and then disappear, but for that to work, I need a supply of grenades. I'll have to teleport to CIA headquarters and get a backpack of grenades. Is there anything else we want?"

"I'd rather have the drone drop something on them, but that can be pretty hard as the boat is moving so the drone has to be low so that it can't miss."

"But won't they just shoot it out of the sky? I would think you'd lose the drone on your first mission," Michelle said. "Have you ever sailed through pirate-infested waters before?"

"Not really, but I've been in many hazardous situations with the CIA. I like the concept of the landing on the ship only long enough to pull the pin on a grenade and then return to this boat, but a lot of things could happen to you during those two to three seconds that you are aboard a pirate vessel."

"I suppose this is something we need to worry about night and day? Does your navigation system have an alert for anything that looks suspicious on the radar? Or will we need to take shifts watching for trouble?"

"I will set the software up to alarm for things on the radar, but you're right that we'll need to be vigilant twenty-four-seven until we reach the Venezuelan mainland. We can do some practice with the drone right now so we know what its capabilities are, and how much time you will have to teleport to a boat and back. Depending on incoming ships to this island that the drone spots, you might try landing on a particular boat, take the pin out of an imaginary grenade, and return to this boat."

"Okay, I'll text Sheila so she gets some stuff ready for when I pop into Langley. Let's get that drone of yours going."

Jason went below and grabbed what looked to be a briefcase and brought it up on deck. He assembled the drone in under five minutes, and they practiced moving it around as well as keeping it high in the sky. It was harder to hear the drone when it was higher in the air and it would be harder to shoot it down. They discussed the boats that appeared to be navigating toward the harbor. Michelle wanted to try landing on a boat with no more than two people on it who hopefully had their backs turned to where Michelle planned to stand. They found the boat they liked, and Michelle vanished in front of Jason's eyes.

No sooner had he blinked a few times than she was back.

"That was quick," Jason said.

"I don't believe the people aboard the boat saw me. I did as you suggested and pulled an imaginary pin from an imaginary grenade, tossed it on the deck, and came back here. How long was I gone? Did you watch me through the drone camera?"

"The drone camera videoed your brief visit, but you were quick. I really didn't have time to look at my watch and judge the amount of time you were gone."

"Can you think of any other weapons to use against these guys? I presume the grenade would kill them and I'd much rather just disable the boat so the motor doesn't work and they get stuck in the middle of the Caribbean Sea."

"From what I've heard about pirates in this area, they like to use old cigar boats. I say *old* because most Venezuelans can't afford to keep them updated, so it should be shabby-looking. They should have fairly powerful motors at the back of the boat. I could give you a pair of wire cutters and you could cut the fuel or electrical switch on the motor. That would take more time, and the men probably wouldn't die stranded out on the sea. Surely someone would come by and rescue their sorry asses."

"Okay, train me how to sabotage the motor, and I'll take a grenade with me for backup."

Jason nodded, and with the practice completed, they discussed a few more items before Michelle called Sheila to arrange a pickup of weapons and then teleported back to Curaçao. Before they came into the Venezuelan port, Michele would have to likely move the weapons off the boat. She would discuss that with Jason later. Rumor had it that the military searched any arriving pleasure boats. This was going to be a much harder scheme to pull off than she had realized. She was vaguely aware of the geopolitical circumstances of most of the world. It was hard not to be as an employee of the CIA but this plan seemed fraught with holes. When Jason had first mentioned the plan, she had somehow envisioned they would be one of many sailing ships to visit the port. Now she understood that they would likely have to engage and kill sea pirates and there would be few leisure boats like theirs and they didn't speak fluent Spanish. She could think of a thousand holes in this plan. Was this the best the agency could do? She raised those questions to her partner before she left.

"Are you comfortable with this plan? I see so many holes in it that I can imagine us in a Venezuelan jail or dead on the open seas. Why couldn't we fly into Colombia and go overland toward Caracas? Or fly into beautiful downtown Caracas on a flight from Panama? We have fake identities, but by appearance, we look like Americans. The idea that we'll just sort of hang out at the docks and hear gossip seems far-fetched. Is there just one dock where we might find the Iranian ship? What if we pick the wrong dock? It seems like the CIA should be better able to handle this situation with an unmanned drone or satellite checking out the ships. This feels like the agency hasn't thought through this plan very well. It feels even vaguer than their last plan of 'go search the world for uranium enrichment centrifuges,'" Michelle said with concern and frustration in her voice.

"While you were saving the world on our last case somewhere in Tahiti, this issue began to surface. We looked at the latest intelligence out of Venezuela. Simply arriving on an airplane from somewhere wouldn't do the trick; the CIA felt that there are too many guards at the airports mostly because there are so many dissenters to President Maduro. We had two case officers arrested last year. So, we felt that simply flying into the airport was a bad idea. We looked at going overland from Colombia, but it is difficult to maintain cover over the two weeks it would take to reach the key docks. A bigger problem was the reason we have to hang out at the docks—the boat gives us that excuse. We don't have the luxury of time that we do with many operations; the ships could be within launch distance soon. Also, these docks are not where a tourist hangs out. The analyst studied the digital images that the satellites were picking up as well as those that the drone took when they flew over the ships. In the case of the drone, the Iranian ship detected it and attempted to shoot it down. We got the drone back, but we noted to pay better attention to the Iranians and not get lazy about the damn thing."

"How about the pirates? Did you discuss that we might have to kill people on the way into this country?"

"Yes. We won't be killing innocents. It's them or us. Perhaps we'll be left alone on the open seas. Certainly, I'll do my best to be invisible and avoid other ships."

"When I signed on to the CIA, I made it clear that I wouldn't be an assassin. It would be too easy for me to pop up in spots around the world, pull a gun out of my pocket, and eliminate someone. That's not who I am or how I operate. This feels like I'm violating my principles."

"So, what's your plan to complete this mission?" Jason asked. He'd thought they came up with the best plan possible, but he didn't want to be working with a partner who had doubts about the plan.

"I don't know. I'd rather strand these pirates out here in the middle of nowhere. How do we explain if we make it alive to the dock? Won't the Venezuelans be suspicious about that?"

"No. It's a big sea out there and it's quite possible that we could make it ashore with no pirate encounters."

Michelle sighed and thought about the operation and what she would recommend that they do differently. Really, if she could leave the folks stranded at sea, she would be fine.

"Let me practice removing the engine part," she said.

"Okay, we'll practice with this boat and another one over there," Jason said pointing to another boat at a different dock. "That boat has the other type of connection between the gas tank and engine I think you might run into. The difficult thing will be landing on the boat. It will take the guys some time to react as it's so unbelievable when you appear out of thin air. Hopefully, by the time they raise their guns, you'll be long gone."

"How about if I just use a knife to cut something?"

"That might work as well. I'll show you two options."

They spent the next thirty minutes practicing until she was able to disable the boat in under five seconds. Jason then borrowed a powerboat so she could practice landing in a moving boat. She was knocked forward each time as she appeared in a static position while the boat was moving forward. Finally, after much practice, she had the hang of it.

"I'm glad I've never tried teleporting into an airplane. I'd hate to be slammed to the back of the plane."

Jason smiled and replied, "These exercises that we've been doing for the past hour should prepare you for just about anything, and you have the timing down to under five seconds. We'll have advance warning of any pirate boats as they will show up on our radar. We'll guide the drone over and see what we have. They like to attack at night, so we'll do three-hour shifts around the clock once we get within fifty miles of the coast. Fortunately, there are more attacks toward Trinidad and Tobago than where we are sailing. Do you think you could bring a rocket launcher back with you?"

"Jason, you're not giving me confidence in my decision to stay with this mission. I've never used a rocket launcher and the only grenades I've pulled the pin on are flashbangs and I haven't done that in perhaps a decade. Besides, aren't the authorities going to be suspicious of this nice-looking boat? Who sails a nice-looking boat to Venezuela?"

"We've been over this, and you haven't thought of an alternative other than aborting the mission which isn't an option."

"Why don't I just teleport to the ship now and see what's up? At this point, it seems to be a safer alternative than this absurd plan. I'm ready to call Sheila, are you?"

"Sure." Jason didn't like going on a mission with a reluctant partner. He couldn't blame her to some degree as this was one of the flakier planned missions he'd been assigned to in his career. But as far as he was concerned, uncertainty was a part of every assignment as a spy. Michelle didn't like undercover work, and this was an undercover job. He'd been dropped in bad areas before, so the potential fight with pirates didn't bother him. He and Michelle were well-armed, or they would be once Michelle made a few trips back to Langley. That was a hole in the original planning for this mission; he should have figured out how to get arms to Curaçao before they left.

# CHAPTER 4

"*H*i Sheila," Michelle said, looking at her phone screen. "I'm freaked out over this plan for our mission, and I wanted to talk through alternatives with you and Jason."

"Yes?" Sheila said, making it clear that she didn't have hope for alternative plans.

"I don't like the plan as it's drawn up at the moment. I guess when I signed onto this mission, I didn't understand how dangerous this part of the world is. I'm worried that Jason isn't going to make it out of here alive. For myself, I have ways to prevent that outcome. Why don't you send me detailed pictures of the ship you took with a drone or satellite, and I'll go check it out. I'll look for the missiles. Jason can stay planted here in Bonaire, and this mission will conclude much faster."

"We debated doing that at the outset of this mission, but as it is sitting in African waters at the moment, we have no reason to intercede with the ships. We need it to sail toward Venezuela."

"True . . . but if I take a look now, you'll know if you have any worries about the ship's contents and you can send the US military after the ship while it's in international waters before it reaches Venezuela."

"We still don't have the right to stop the ship."

"Then what were you going to do in Venezuela? Have Jason and me secretly attack the missiles? Because the military certainly can't make an armed attack in that country."

Sheila picked up on the fact that Michelle was vehemently opposed to the mission she was assigned to. That wasn't a good thing in a case officer. Errors were made when officers weren't committed. She sighed. She would have loved to just order Michelle to follow the assignment, but that wasn't the way she led her people. Besides, Michelle had saved the world on her last assignment and Sheila owed her more than she could ever repay.

"We don't have a lot of good options here. We also have poor intelligence in this case. We really don't know that we have a problem with these ships. We do have a problem with Venezuela that we have so far failed to fix. I was hoping to kill two birds with one stone. We could use you as a listening device in that country if we could figure out where to plant you. You are perhaps the one case officer who could stay safe in that volatile country. We closed our embassy there two years ago and the country is becoming increasingly violent and desperate. What will their impact be on the United States? We just don't know."

"And for that, you're willing to risk Jason's life? If I'm arrested I can disappear before any harm is done. He can't. We need to change this mission. I'll go check the ships out, which will give you the answers you need for military support by Iran for Venezuela. As to what else is going on in that country, can you be more specific? The likelihood that I could just eavesdrop in the right place at the right time to hear critical intelligence is a fantasy."

Sheila felt herself losing control of this vague and tenuous mission. When she discussed it with her superiors and the analysts, this was the best they were able to come up with, but she'd known that it was a weak plan.

Jason had heard enough and decided it was time to make his opinion known.

"Sheila, Michelle neither likes nor feels talented at undercover work. I have had many missions that start out just as vague as this one and I'm not worried about it. I think we can win any contest with pirates we may come into contact with as we approach the Venezuelan coast. We'll win as Michelle will spend some time obtaining weapons for our boat. She's learned how to disable their boat engines to leave them adrift.

"As to something else going on in the country, I agree with both of you. Michelle is right that thinking we can just show up at the right place and overhear something pertinent is not believable. On the other hand, we need to gain some intelligence. Can your analysts do some more work and give us a more specific location? We'll have to run the gauntlet of the Venezuelan military when we approach the coast and they can make unpredictable demands. Should they detain us, Michelle can leave at a moment's notice while I'll end up in custody. Michelle can sneak into wherever I'm detained and slip me the weapons to get out. It won't be the first time I've spent some time in custody at the behest of a foreign government."

"What if they harm or torture you?" Michelle asked.

"Just know that they'll try and that you'll need to move fast."

"But what if I don't know where you are? How can I help you? Why are you willing to make the ultimate sacrifice over this assignment? We don't know if ICBMs exist or what crackpot scheme Venezuela has planned, but whatever it is, it requires more planning."

"I don't think we have the luxury of waiting while we figure out a new plan, and I frankly don't think there is a better plan. One of the things I've learned over my years with the CIA is that some of the vaguest, poorly planned operations yield the best results if you make it out alive. I'll wear a GPS device in a few places so that you will know where to find me."

Michelle realized that as bad and vague the plan was, Jason and Sheila were still ready to move on it. She thought it likely that even if she resigned from the mission Jason would still go through with it and probably get himself killed. She'd have to stay close just to make sure he got out alive. She would have to think about her commitment to the agency after this mission. When she worked alone rescuing hostages, she didn't have to worry about the safety of a partner. If she and Jason were partners going forward, that added a whole other layer of tension to these operations.

Michelle capitulated and nodded her agreement with the plan, and the call ended shortly after. Sheila needed time to gather the weapons that Michelle and Jason would need before she expected to see Michelle in person in her office. Later Jason stored a variety of weapons all over the boat, and they were ready to leave early the next morning. With a little more discussion, they headed to their respective beds for the last good sleep before the perilous part of the mission started.

The next morning just before dawn, they set their radar heading south and toward the Venezuelan coast. They were taking turns navigating the boat and watching for pirates. They turned off the AIS system so their boat wouldn't be sending out signals to other boats. Jason removed the radar beacon on the top of the mast. It was a sunny, clear day which made it easier for pirates to see their sails, but the sea was calm. Michelle would take a calm sea and potentially more pirates over horrible weather which would have her puking her guts out. What did that say about her when she thought fighting pirates was easier than fighting seasickness?

It was nighttime as they approached the coast and surprisingly it had been a quiet day. No boats headed their way; now all they needed was the final thirty minutes of this cruise to be equally quiet. Sometimes the most dangerous area was the mile in front of the marina. They were both on deck ready for bad actors to come their way.

Jason was standing at the front and said, "We have a suspicious boat coming at us from one o'clock."

Michelle nodded and replied, "Launching the drone."

She navigated the drone toward one o'clock, searching for the boat. Attached to the drone was a smoke bomb that would quickly block the sight of whoever was in the approaching boat. Within thirty seconds she located the inflatable boat, verified that they were likely bad actors, and then lowered the drone and dropped the smoke bomb into the raft. She then changed course for the sailboat to avoid an accidental collision as there was a lot of conversation coming from the inflatable.

"Great job, Captain," Jason murmured from his position at the boat's front railing.

"Is that it or is there a second boat of pirates out there?"

"I think that would be it. It wouldn't make sense that two groups of pirates would fight over the harbor every night, especially when traffic approaching the marina is rare at this hour."

She could hear sounds behind them as the inflatable boat fought its way clear of the smoke with little success. They switched positions with Michelle acting as the scout while Jason used his nautical skills to bring their sailboat into the marina. Jason had a reservation for a slip, but he was expecting trouble as the marinas rarely had foreign boat visitors and the Venezuelan versions of customs and border patrol were known to work almost purely on bribery. Their sailboat had two flags—Venezuelan and Panamanian. The Venezuelan flag was a courtesy to the host country, the Panamanian flag was to match the information on their passports.

Without further incidents, Michelle was soon jumping from the sailboat to the dock to tie down the boat while they dealt with the official paperwork for the marina and for the country. Much of the work would continue the next day as the government offices were closed for the day. They confirmed their slip space and moved the boat to its resting spot for the next week or so. They both were on alert for any whispered conversations regarding the boat they had smoke-bombed but heard nothing. They set their security system for the night and retired. Jason had installed motion detectors, lights, and cameras to protect the boat. Their weapons were locked away underneath the boat below a false bottom in a watertight container. If the authorities came aboard to inspect their boat, they wanted to make sure that if they brought sniffer dogs with them, they wouldn't be able to smell any weapons.

They were down below summarizing their day in an email for Sheila. They knew they would waste much of the next day dealing with the port authorities, after which they would begin trying to infiltrate the country. Michelle felt like an uneven partner; she could save Jason's life in many ways, but if he needed her to act a certain way to glean information, she might fail the mission before they started.

"I think we were lucky not to encounter any pirates until nearly the end."

"Yes, and I'm happy we could block their bad behavior without any bloodshed or attention for us. But let's not jinx ourselves and celebrate too early."

"Do you think they got close enough to this boat to know what we look like? Is it a danger for it to be sitting at a marina?"

"I think we're okay. From what I've read,- these pirates don't originate out of the main harbors or marinas, so I don't think they were close enough to get a description of our boat. Of course, they could probably assume this is where we were heading, but hopefully, they're still coughing from the smoke bomb and we'll hear them before they get here."

"You're full of cheery thoughts."

"Yeah, we've just begun to run the Venezuelan gauntlet and I'll admit I'm not looking forward to dealing with their officials tomorrow. Sometimes, they detain you just for the hell of it. We're going to be hit with fees and we can't argue too much. I'll want to scream that they are full of bull poop, but instead, we'll just pretend that sailing is our passion and that is why we're visiting their ports."

Michelle sighed and leaned back against the hull. "After we get clearance to be in port, where are we going to go next? Are we staying here to listen to the gossip or are we moving east to bigger marinas?"

"We don't want to move too soon as we have a multiple-day slip rental, but over the next few days, we'll hang out in restaurants near this harbor and see if we can gather any intel."

"I still can't believe we're in a dangerous country running on such a flimsy plan. You're sure that our weapons can't be found? That's the fast path to prison or death."

"Our lab people swear that the box will block all odors and the inspectors would seriously have to take this boat apart to find it in the first place. I'm not worried. The guards aren't that talented at finding contraband. They are much more worried about maximizing their bribes. Let's not worry about pirates or Venezuelan police for the moment and instead focus on what else is going on in this country. The word on the street is something is about to happen, but no one has a guess as to what it is. I somehow don't think that the buzz is about ICBMs. That wouldn't be worthy of our time here."

"Given the chaos here, I would suggest that only two things could cause a buzz among the population—money or power. The ICBMs might create a cash flow for the Venezuelans, but not long term, and that's not likely to reach many people. Probably only those high up in the government will benefit from a stand-off with the United States over rockets. Of course, that's assuming our country just doesn't bomb them into oblivion."

"True, so maybe it's money. This country has a lot of natural resources, but there are embargoes against their export because of the government. So, what other stuff can they sell?" Jason asked.

"Illicit drugs? Does Colombia send cocaine directly to the United States or do they route it through Venezuela or Panama perhaps?"

"Maybe. Look, you better take a nap. I've got the first shift and so I'll see you in the morning."

They said their goodnights and began taking turns, guarding the boat from whatever night creatures might want to step aboard. It was going to be a long couple of weeks before this mission was over.

# CHAPTER 5

*A*s Jason predicted, the harbor and immigration authorities were focused on one thing only—how much could they fleece the Americans for? Michelle was glad that Jason did the negotiations as she lacked patience for the corrupt officials. She had fantasies of appearing behind each of them just long enough to take a swing at their heads. Holding onto that fantasy kept her sanity. The entire day was lost to those negotiations and permits. Finally, they were finished by the time the evening meal rolled around. Now it was time to go to work on the CIA's mission. Overnight, the analysts had gathered new information on the three Iranian ships, and it looked as though Michelle would be able to visit the three ships in the next day or two to see what was on board.

While doing the corrupt government official shuffle, they had kept their eyes open for places to eat and drink near the port. They were looking for a place seemingly filled with sailors and stevedores in hopes that they could listen to the gossip of the port staff.

"Have you been sent on other missions where you've had to just listen for gossip?" Michelle asked over a glass of rum and coke. It was quite tasty, and she could see that she would be drunk in no time if she had a few more of the delicious drinks.

"All the time. Sometimes having boots on the ground is all we need to uncover some piece of information that's bad for the United States. Are you having any trouble understanding what people are saying in Spanish?"

"I've been able to pretty much follow the entire conversation. I understand about eighty to ninety percent of their words and I can fill in the missing words in a sentence. The accent is different from what I hear in California, but otherwise, my comprehension is pretty good. How's your Spanish doing?"

"I think you might be better than me. I kept feeling like I was a sentence behind. Of course, I was also trying to act like I spoke minimal Spanish so they would drop their guard in front of us, but that didn't seem to work. They must be used to visitors playing that game."

Their meals arrived and they continued to chat while also trying to listen to the conversations around them. Neither heard anything of significance. They also put feelers out as to where the Iranian ships might dock. Of course, they couldn't ask the question outright, but there were sly ways to ease into the question.

"We're not getting anywhere. Let's head back to our boat," Jason said, after paying their bill.

They were halfway between their boat and the restaurant when they felt three men approach them from the back. One of the men said in Spanish that he wanted their money and their watches.

Michelle whispered, "I'll take two of them out with a kick to the back of their knees. I'll leave the third one closest to the port for you."

Jason nodded and a short minute later, they left three men groaning on the ground as they continued their stroll toward the boat. Once aboard, they set their usual alarms and leaned against the hull as they spoke.

"I'm really hating this country. Between the corrupt officials, desperate people, and criminal minds, it's hard to see any natural beauty. I need to study these photos and decide where I'm going aboard the ship. I've never searched a ship before, and I know there are all kinds of compartments. So if I'm not efficient, I could end up spending a lot of time aboard and in view of cameras. Have you stepped on an enemy ship in your career?"

Jason thought for a moment then shook his head.

"Unless someone has your teleportation skill, it would be extremely dangerous to do that. First, if you're out to sea, there's nowhere to go. So, you can't run away. The corridors are skinny and unless you have the ship's blueprint memorized, it's easy to get lost. Finally, bullets ricochet around the metal of the ship so you can die accidentally, which in my mind is a stupid way to die."

Michelle held out a photo and pointed to a door on the deck. "Should I start here?"

"I'd ask the analysts to plot a course for you. Maybe they can consult someone in our Navy concerning the best way to navigate the ship."

"That's an excellent suggestion. I'll do that."

They heard voices outside and the camera focused on the dock was activated by the motion of people outside. Michelle and Jason watched through the camera lens to assess what was going on. There were two men on the dock in the dark; neither had anything official looking on their clothes like a badge, nameplate, or uniform.

"They appear to be more criminals," Michelle said. "Should I pop in back of them and give them a shove into the water?"

"I could go out and talk to them," Jason offered.

"I see guns. One guy is holding one in his hand and the other has his tucked in his waistband. Let's not give them the chance to put a few holes in you. I like the idea of shoving them in the water as that makes their guns inoperable once they get water into them."

"True. I feel like a lazy partner while you go out and fight the battles. We're going to have to figure out some balance here. You'll have to let me take a few guys out."

"Just get used to it. I can take these guys out without breaking a sweat, and better still, they never know what happened to them. Besides, it makes my day to do these thugs in. I'll be right back," Michelle said, uncurling from her seated position.

Jason continued watching on his monitor as first one guy than the other was soon spin-wheeling their way into the water. Michelle had managed to push them into an area with no ladders back to the dock, and the planks of the dock were too high for the men to use to leverage their way out of the water. Michelle returned to the deck of their sailboat to admire her handiwork. Then she returned to her seated position leaning against the hull.

She looked at her watch and said, "I dispatched those two idiots in less than a minute. Best of all, they don't feel revengeful toward us or this boat as they don't know that we were the cause of their late evening swim. Each time I take out one of these thugs, I release a little of the frustration of dealing with these corrupt officials."

"So you're saying I should continue to let you take the lead defending this boat as it is a mental health treatment for you?"

"Yeah, shoving those fools into the water was better than the awesome rum and coke I had earlier at the restaurant. If these men could time it right, I could have daily therapy until this operation is at an end," she said with a smile.

Jason grinned and added, "You are the oddest partner I've had in nearly thirty years with the agency. In many ways, you're the best case officer ever, and then there's this huge hole in your skillset wherein you have zero acting ability. In some ways it's amazing you chose the clandestine service when you're so bad at acting."

"You're the only partner I've had, so I don't know if you're good or bad in the eyes of other agents, but I know you have my back and that's what really matters."

The boat's cameras picked up more movement and Jason said, "I guess that's our cue to end the sappy conversation and get back to the dangerous world that's Venezuela."

"Are the guys back from their swim?" Michelle asked while watching Jason move the boat's cameras.

"I don't see what triggered the alarm. . . . Oh, there it is. Looks like we have a new group."

Michelle rubbed her hands together and said, "I can't wait. This is better than cardio at working out the kinks. Be back in a second."

Jason walked up the stairs to the boat deck to get a bird's eye view of Michelle in action. He was in dark clothing, and they had no lights in the area where he was standing, so he was safe from any random gunfire. He had to avoid a full-throttle smile knowing his teeth would gleam in the moonlight as he heard successive splashes in the water followed by curses in Spanish. One of the men overboard couldn't swim and his two friends were fully occupied saving him. Jason jumped a little when Michelle appeared beside him.

"I'm warming up to this country. If I can continue shoving criminals into the water and destroying their guns while I'm at it, then that's quality work for a CIA case officer."

"Indeed. I will say that I hope this is it for the night as we need some sleep at some point. Perhaps, I should talk to the marina office about security tomorrow."

"I'm getting very cynical about this country, and I have to wonder if the marina office is calling these thugs over because we look like easy pickings. There's one other visiting boat so maybe we could put a new lock on the gate down to docks and share the key with them."

"I'm not sure what is going on with that boat. I haven't seen any human activity over there—legal or criminal."

"Perhaps they're brave enough souls to have explored the interior," Michelle suggested.

"Perhaps. I'm tempted to board their boat and see what's going on. Perhaps it's a decoy to make visitors like ourselves feel safer because another boat is in port."

"I hadn't thought of that. Why don't I go over right now and see what is up? Is the layout the same as this boat?"

Jason looked over and replied, "It should be, but why don't you start on top and see if the door is locked to the cabin. That will tell us something."

Michelle nodded and disappeared. Jason squinted in the distance and could just see her shadow aboard the distant sailboat. Then she disappeared again, and Jason wondered if she walked or teleported through the cabin door. Before he finished thinking about it, she appeared next to him.

"The boat is completely empty. There were no clothes or food. I wonder if the government confiscated the boat or perhaps it is as you suggested, just a decoy to get us to let our guard down? Regardless, let's go put another lock on the fence as that will hold off the visitors for the remainder of the night. We'll also have to think about a few triggers to dissuade any visitors while we're gone tomorrow."

They soon had a new lock on the dock gate that resulted in a quiet night in which they both got a sound sleep. Michelle could've gone back to the hotel in Curaçao, but the water was smooth in the marina, and she felt the need to be close by for Jason.

On the way into town the next morning, they stopped by the marina office to notify them of the new lock as the one that was there was apparently not working. At first, the port officials asked for it to be removed, but they couldn't offer a better alternative for securing Jason and Michelle's boat. Jason left his cell number and told management that they were visiting historic sites in the city, but in reality, they spent the entire morning exploring all the nooks and crannies of the port desperately looking for information before returning to their pier with lunch in hand.

"I don't think there is any reason to stay here," Michelle said after their morning's activities.

"I have to agree with you. Either the information we seek is hidden or it's not here. Regardless, there seems no point in staying."

"I'm exploring the Iranian ships this evening as soon as it gets dark where the ships are located. You shouldn't sail in this part of the world without me. I don't think we can leave this port until tomorrow morning."

"Good point. I'll do the checkout later today so we can sail at first light without worrying about upsetting the government officials."

The remainder of the day was non-eventful with no new criminals lining up to visit their boat. The Iranian ships were at about the same latitude and the CIA case officers were across the Atlantic Ocean from each other. As dusk set in, Michelle, dressed in all black and teleported to the largest Iranian ship. Her immediate assessment was that she teleported to a quiet place aboard the ship. She saw no one walking around or guarding the boat deck near where she had made an appearance. She would have to remember to thank the analysts for targeting this location. Now she needed to move down levels of the ship to determine what the ship was holding. The CIA estimated that the Iranian navy had at least one-hundred men aboard, so she knew she had to be careful.

She used her teleporting skill to move around the ship rather than taking corridors and ladders at a regular pace. In her experience, people were more willing to doubt themselves and what they saw if she appeared and disappeared. She also practiced a few lines in Farsi just to further scare the crewmen. Basically, she planned to say that she was the siren from the sea, and they should jump overboard. If that didn't work, she would try being "Pairaka" who in Persian literature was a female sorceress and demon. Surely, they would be afraid of her? That was her game plan, but as she was such a bad actress, she wasn't sure she would think of these ideas when the moment presented itself.

She had a camera attached to her black beanie that was filming her progress through the ship. She wondered what the analysts thought when she suddenly changed from one level or room to another. They probably thought she was turning the camera off and on. Alas, that was not the case.

She reached the third level down and thought she heard someone coming. She looked for a place to hide but saw nothing. She decided she would wait until someone appeared and then step behind them. That worked fine, as by the time the crewman reacted to her presence, she moved behind him. He moved forward, looking in the room behind her and up a stairway. He turned a flashlight on to look in the well-lit room which made Michelle chuckle silently. She continued to listen for other approaching crewmen, but she just had this one to contend with. Eventually, he mumbled to himself and climbed the stairs to the next level. She let out a sigh and continued to explore the ship's contents.

She had a few other encounters that were benign as long as she moved out of their way. She found military equipment like guns, bullets, rockets, and even a helicopter or two. She didn't find anything the size of an ICBM, nor did she find rocket fuel. Venezuela was known for its large petroleum reserves and probably could make its own rocket fuel. She visited one room that was puzzling to her. The information on the side of what looked to her to be canisters or mini rockets was in a foreign language which she assumed was Farsi. She knew it wasn't any of the romance languages, nor an Asian language, but beyond that, she couldn't guess.

She pulled her phone out and shot some pictures just to be sure she had this area on film. She checked her watch and saw she had been aboard the ship for an hour. It was time to go. She was really pressing her luck staying aboard much longer. She was surprised she hadn't triggered any cameras, or maybe the people watching weren't paying attention or maybe they couldn't believe what they were seeing. Regardless, a moment later she was in the hotel room in Curaçao. She debated going back to the sailboat, but she wanted to make sure the coast was clear before she did that, and frankly the Wi-Fi was more secure and faster in Curaçao.

She uploaded the camera footage from her beanie camera and the single shots from her phone. Then she called Sheila.

"Did you see my footage, especially the last area I visited with the canisters?"

"Yes, we're translating the wording now. One of the analysts assigned to this case speaks Farsi and that's the language we think we are looking at."

Michelle heard a conversation in Sheila's background and her anxiety ratcheted up.

"Did someone in your background just say that the words on those canisters translated to mustard gas?"

"Yes, you heard correctly. We've got a problem. The Geneva Protocol signed in 1925-- almost one-hundred years ago, bans the use of chemical weapons. There is no reason for Iran to be transporting cylinders with a mustard gas label across the Atlantic Ocean. If their excuse is that they are disposing of these agents, then they are not following established protocols. Those canisters could be dropped by planes or helicopters or drones on any population. I'm going to have to consult with my superiors to plan what to do next. We'll likely need to send you back to the ship. We're probably going to need to sink that ship and it would be good to know if those weapons are located in an airtight part of the ship. It would mean less damage to marine life as the ship rests on the bottom of the Atlantic Ocean."

"How about the two other ships? Do I need to explore those?"

"That's a good question. We weren't aware of any large stores of mustard gas by the Iranians. I'm no chemist, but I think it has to be easy to make. We're going to need you to check out those other ships and see what cargo they have."

"Any suggestions from the analysts on where I should board the ship or where I might want to look, or any blueprints for these two other ships?"

"We hadn't asked those questions up to this point because we were looking for ICBMs. Now that we're looking for something else, something much smaller, I'll see what we can come up with," Sheila said looking at her watch. "It's approaching one in the morning in the region where the ships are located. I'll see if we can come up with something in the next hour or so to enable you to get back there tonight."

"Okay. I'm staying in the suite in Curaçao. Call me when you have the directions of what I should be looking for. I'm going to check in with Jason to make sure he doesn't need any help. We have been averaging two to three attacks a day since we arrived in Venezuela. I'll make sure he's safe without me there to push the criminals and their guns into the water," Michelle said with a smile.

"That is a handy skillset you have there, Michelle," Sheila said. "I'll get back to you within a few hours."

Michelle checked her watch, and it was coming up at eleven at night. She called Jason to see how he was doing.

"Did you discover anything on the ships?" Jason asked once they connected.

"It appears the Iranians are carrying canisters of mustard gas. I'm being sent back to visit the two smaller ships to see what cargo they're carrying. How are you doing? Any more criminals approaching the boat?"

"I've dispatched one group tonight. I used the drone to drop pepper spray on them. One of them fell into the water because of course, they couldn't see. The other two crawled back toward the gate. Unfortunately, there seems to be a never-ending supply of desperate Venezuelans. I've got the boat covered through the night. Do you think you'll be back on board tomorrow? I'd rather leave port with you aboard in case anyone's watching."

"I should hear of my target by midnight our time, which is two in the morning where the Iranian ships are located. I'll take no more than an hour per ship. That should put me back on board at three or four in the morning. We're moving the boat to the port at Caracas?"

"Close by. It's a more industrial port. A city by the name of La Guaria. Container ships are unloaded there and it's just one of two container ports for the country. Surely we will hear some good gossip there."

"Is there a place for us to park at that port?"

"I guess I have no hope of teaching you Mariners' language. We don't park boats, we navigate into a slip. Back to your question. There's isn't room for a boat like ours there. I've rented a slip at a nearby marina. It will take less than two hours to move, but we'll be under constant attack, I think."

"Oh joy. Tell me the waves will be relatively smooth."

"Well, look at the bright side: you get a normal shower before returning to the boat. That's more than I get."

"True. I'm also doing my laundry while I'm here. At some point, I'll bring your clothes back to Curaçao so you get clean laundry too."

"There is that to look forward to. See you in a few hours."

"Stay safe. If you think you need my help, don't hesitate to call. I can disappear from the Iranian boats long enough to dispatch a few people before returning to the middle of the Atlantic Ocean."

"As I said earlier, you're a woman of many interesting skills. Buenos noches."

"Good night."

# CHAPTER 6

$\mathcal{M}$ ichelle had managed two laundry loads and had time to hang them outside to dry before Langley called again. It didn't matter that it was dark outside; it was still warm enough to dry clothes.

"What do you have for me?" Michelle asked.

"As you can imagine, there is quite a dance going on here in Washington. We have a Seal team that will be launched from an atomic submarine to sink those Iranian ships. Better still, we have a tropical storm developing in the area where the ships are headed, so we can use that for cover when they sink."

"That's good news. Do you have maps and suggestions for me about checking out the smaller ships?"

"We do. We're transmitting them now. Once you explore those ships, we'll put together our plan to sink one or more ships of this flotilla."

Michelle used a separate computer to open the files with the ship blueprints, and comments by the analysts regarding where to board, crewmen numbers, and suggestions on where to look for any additional chemicals.

Michelle studied the materials and then told Sheila she was off to explore the ships after donning her dark clothing and beanie cap camera.

"Good luck. I hope you quickly find evidence of mustard gas on the other two ships. It makes it easier to have three ships mysteriously disappear, rather than take down one ship and have observers on two other ships."

"I'll keep that in mind."

Michelle made her preparations and soon found herself in the middle of the Atlantic on a ship that was rolling in a few more waves than the bigger Iranian ship. She found the waves unnerving even though she intellectually knew that they weren't big waves as the ship was not yet close to the tropical storm. That gave her added incentive to find evidence of something worth destroying the ship for. If she didn't find it quickly, she would be leaving evidence of vomit all over the ship. She moved as fast as she could, making some weird landings depending on the pitch of the vessel. The analysts suggested that the majority of the men would be asleep as it was the middle of the night. Either they were sleeping in hammocks that swayed with the ship or they were somehow strapped into their beds. She guessed that was a question for another day.

Michelle was so fast-moving around the ship that she accidentally slammed into a crew member rounding a corner. She quickly moved elsewhere before the man had time to confirm that he'd run into an obstruction. If time wasn't so important, she would have been tempted to stay around and see how the man looked for her. However, she was here to search the ship and she needed to stay on mission. She continued on her memorized path to the cargo hold areas of the ship that might contain chemical weapons or something else equally bad.

She reached one of two large cargo rooms but found they were filled with transportation vehicles, helicopters, drones, and a single small airplane. At least now they knew how they planned to disperse the mustard gas canisters. However, none of these vehicles would reach the US mainland, so perhaps their target was a Venezuelan neighbor like Colombia or Brazil.

She briefly returned to her suite in Curaçao, uploaded the footage, and returned to the second ship. It was so shocking to leave the peace, quiet, and heat of the Caribbean and be thousands of miles due east encountering the cold, dark, and windy Atlantic. Again, she made her way through the ship heading for the cargo hold. This third ship was even smaller than the other two and was really being tossed about in the waves. She found a life vest in a corridor of the boat and put it on. She could see herself getting hit by a huge wave and going overboard. She could only hope that she would be alert before the big wave hit to get the heck off the ship and back to her dry hotel room.

She continued toward the cargo hold without running into any crewman. She knew she would have a few bruises tomorrow as she was slammed into walls and sharp objects with the ship's movement. It was a perfect time to secretly explore the enemy's ship as no one was about at this hour of bad weather. She was on the verge of puking, but kept telling herself to hold on for another five minutes. She found the entry door to the cargo hold and teleported behind it. There were dim lights on, which helped her avoid serious injury from a pallet that was sliding back and forth with the ship. Some crew person forgot to secure it. She jumped aboard the sliding pallet and nearly tossed her cookies as she slid across the floor and then slammed into the other wall. She opened a box on the pallet to find it loaded with guns and ammo. This was a bad pallet to be sliding as the waves were supposed to get worse and the pallet would break up on one of the wall hits. Given the metal walls of the ship, if the ammo broke free of the boxes, it might explode from friction and force. She paused and tried to think of all the gun safety classes she had taken over the years, but could think of no specific reference to the situation she was in. She made quick work of the other boxes and saw nothing of concern to US interests. It was time to head back to Curaçao.

A moment later she was grabbing onto the wall in the hotel suite as she felt like she was still riding the waves inside the boat. Once her dizziness abated enough for her to see straight, she walked into the kitchen for some ginger ale to sip while she uploaded the new information to Langley.

It was three in the morning, and she figured she would be back with Jason by four. She placed a call to Sheila.

"Did you get my video and photos?"

"We did. That is some wild video. I was seasick watching it; I can only imagine how bad it was aboard the boat."

"Yeah, when I got back to Curaçao, I had to hold onto a doorway until the world stopped spinning. I'm drinking ginger ale and hoping not to puke during our call."

"You nearly died when the pallet slid toward you. Thank goodness for the lights in that cargo hold."

"Yeah, of all the ways to die in this world, being hit by a pallet didn't make my top ten list. It looks like you have reason to destroy all three ships. I was trying to remember my firearms training to determine if the smallest ship will self-destruct once the ammo breaks free and starts slamming into the walls of the cargo hold, but it's beyond my understanding."

"It's beyond my training as well. Your work is done on this part of the mission. We will be sending a different gang to put those three ships down. I'd feel bad about the deaths of perhaps one-hundred-fifty sailors, but the presence of those mustard gas canisters relieves me of any guilt."

"Okay. I'm going to bring my laundry inside and head out to Jason's boat. We're heading to a new marina in the morning."

"Michelle, thanks for sticking with this case. I know you could have resigned or asked to be reassigned. With so many unknowns about Venezuela, it's important having you there to partner with Jason."

"Well, I'm not happy about it, but as I can't come up with a better plan, I'm sticking with Jason. You do know that we were attacked at least three times since we docked in that country?"

"Yeah, you told me earlier. Remind Jason he owes me a few reports."

"Will do. Good night."

Michelle took another twenty minutes to pack her clothes and eat some food. After being tossed about in that small ship, she was happy their boat was parked at a dock in a marina. The waves would be quiet for a few hours when she arrived. Hopefully, she'd catch a little sleep before being forced to go topside due to nausea. She texted Jason about her impending arrival and soon landed on the dock next to the boat. She stepped aboard knowing she was setting off alarms and putting the boat in a rocking motion. She came up the ladder and reached for her bag.

"Do we have a little time for sleep before we set off?"

"We do. I need a few hours of sleep myself. I feel like I've been fighting off bandits all night."

"I've been aboard small vessels rocking side to side all night. I'm so grateful we're parked at a dock."

He gave her a pained look over what Michelle assumed was her lack of nautical terminology, but she was too tired to care. Instead, she searched for some sleeping clothes.

"Wake me up when you need me or at least before we get under-way. I'd hate to wake from a dead sleep with an acute need to barf."

"Will do. I'm going to try and get some shut-eye myself."

"How many groups of criminals did you contend with in my absence?"

"Just one more. I used the drone to drop green dye-colored vinegar on them which dissuaded them from moving closer to the boat."

"Well done! Let's get a little sleep."

By late morning, they were underway to their next port of call. Hopefully, this would prove more informative for the CIA.

"Overall, as a sailor, are you enjoying this trip?" Michelle asked.

"I'm not enjoying sailing the coast of Venezuela. I did enjoy the ABC islands. I'd like to come back on my own boat and scuba some of the areas around those islands."

"ABC?"

"Aruba, Bonaire, and Curaçao," Jason said. "I have no hope of your picking up any nautical language, but you're very capable of watching my six as you cops like to say, we're good."

"Since I discovered seasickness at a young age, sailing in anything more than a giant pool has been on my list of *don't go there*. Oddly, all of my assignments with you have involved the water. Hopefully, our next assignment just involves land."

"You mean you want to partner with me again?" Jason asked, curious about her perception of their missions.

"Yes. I guess I didn't realize how much I missed the camaraderie and partnership of my fellow officers. Yeah, it was satisfying rescuing hostages, but when you have no contact with anyone other than Sheila Meeks, it's an isolating job that feels like you're just punching a timecard. I like planning for 'what-ifs' with someone besides myself. Does that make sense? Is that how you've felt about partners you've had over the years at the agency?"

"I know what you mean about the what-ifs. As a human, I know I have some blind spots or even holes in my brain. Having a second person who is on the ground with you to help with decision-making is better. The fact that you can fetch me an ice-cold beer no matter what hell hole we're in around the world is icing on the cake."

"Ha, so I'm only appreciated for my waitress duties. I'll remind you of the cold beer the next time you need me to rescue you from hypothermia."

"Okay, cold beer and other life-saving things."

"Hmmm, I guess we're making progress in your assessment of my abilities."

"You see anything on the horizon? There are so many blips on the radar screen since we're this close to the shore that I can't tell which boats are pleasure, business, or pirates."

Michelle was sitting at the front of the boat, legs dangling over the edge and arms braced on the railing as she used binoculars to check out individual boats. Between the movement of the boat and the small field of the lens, it was a tough way to look for pirate boats.

"This isn't an efficient way to look for pirate boats. How about if I launch the drone so we can get a bird's eye view of what is going on around us?"

"The battery will probably only last for twenty to thirty minutes. I have backup batteries, but you need to be watching the charge or we're going to lose the drone to the Caribbean Sea."

"Why don't I steer the boat and you use the drone for lookout? I think you're probably more effective with the drone than I am. Do you have our course plotted on the radar screen?"

"I do have our course plotted and that's a great suggestion. Give me a few minutes to get the drone set and we can switch positions."

Michelle continued to search the area looking for pirate ships. It was a good thing that Jason was getting the drone ready. She saw a suspicious boat heading their way. Using the binoculars, she noted men with guns aboard.

"We have inbound unfriendlies coming at three o'clock. Is that drone ready? ETA probably four minutes."

"I'm coming now. Weapons?"

"Of course; that was my definition of unfriendlies. It's not like you can fish with an automatic weapon. Or I guess you can kill fish; you just can't eat them."

"Always good to have a sense of humor about these situations," Jason said as he launched the drone into the sky toward the incoming boat. He flew it up high above the pirate boat and came in behind it.

"What are you going to do with the drone?" Michelle asked from the cockpit of the boat.

"I should have prepared the drone before we left. It's still loaded with the green-colored vinegar. I'm going to come in behind them and try to blind the driver and a few of the shooters with vinegar. It's going to be tricky as I'll have to match the speed of the boat, get low, and not get shot out of the sky. If that fails, I may have to go to plan B, which involves you destroying the motor. I'm just not sure where you can land on the boat. It doesn't look like there is room. So, we need a plan C."

"Fingers crossed. Maybe they'll be distracted by the plight of some of their boat members and I can slip in. Certainly, if you nail the driver that will cause disarray."

Michelle was alternating between steering and checking out the boat with the binoculars. Jason was wildly successful with the drone. He waited for the boat pilot to look up and then sprayed him with the solution. The pirate took his hands off the rudder to wipe his face. Then he must have gotten the idea to wash his eyes out in the sea, so he blindly leaned over and managed to dump the entire boat.

"Bonus points to you for taking the entire ship out at once. What else are you thinking of dropping from the drone? We should outfit it immediately."

"Let's revert to smoke bombs and I was also thinking of something to deflate the inflatable raft-type boats. Wouldn't that be great fun to leave the pirates with a sinking boat? It's a long swim to shore."

"A bow and arrow would be awesome, but can we get the drone to fire it?"

"Not the drone I have."

"Can I fetch you one from Langley?"

"Probably not in time before the next group of pirates moves our way. I'd also need some time to train with it."

"Okay, smoke bombs it is unless I can safely land on the boat and do some damage."

While they were chatting, Jason brought the drone back to the boat. He added another smoke bomb and changed the battery before launching it overhead to check out what was going on.

"More unfriendlies at two o'clock. Crap, there is also a boat at five o'clock. I think you can land on the second boat, take a look."

Michelle used the binoculars to focus on the boat and the motor to verify it was like the one she practiced on with Jason. There were four men in the boat with weapons. All she could hope for was the element of surprise.

"There's no time like the present to see if your plan works. I'll leave the wheel on autopilot and be right back."

Michelle took a deep breath, then imagined the boat she viewed through the binoculars. Her plan was to land at the back, grab the tube connecting the gas tank and the engine and stuff it in her pants pocket, then leave before anyone had the opportunity to fire a gun.

It sort of went that way. She rocked the boat considerably when she landed on it, jamming her hip into the rim and almost going over the edge. She reached for the engine cord piece and had to tug on it twice. The boat slowed down and the men were talking in Spanish, but she didn't waste time concentrating on hearing what they were saying. The cord came free, the boat came to an abrupt halt, and Michelle stuffed the cord in her pocket and was gone. She made a grab for the wheel upon her return to their boat because it was also in motion and she would have lost her balance backward.

"You're back with no injuries?"

"A bruised hip from the rim of the boat, but fortunately they were too slow to react. Their boat is now dead in the water. How's your drone doing?"

"See the smoke in the distance? Coming in from behind seems to do the trick. I can drop the smoke bomb on them before they can shoot it out of the sky, and then the smoke is so bad so quickly that all they can worry about is if the boat is on fire."

"Okay, good job. How soon will we be at our new marina? This is getting tedious."

"We have another hour to go, so my guess is that we will have at least three more pirate boats to contend with."

However, the remainder of their trip was surprisingly uneventful.

"I wonder if word got around about the two boats. Maybe we'll leave this country as legends," Michelle said.

"I'm sure they're talking about a mermaid who came out of the sea to destroy their boat. Can you imagine them explaining that to a law enforcement officer?"

"Wouldn't they have to admit they were pirates, then?"

"True," Jason said, and he steered the boat into their new marina. "Are you ready to play the corrupt official game?"

"How about if I stay aboard the boat? Since we've had two attempted robberies, I need to stay here for protection."

"I think that is a good idea. They'll want to come aboard at some point for "an inspection" so they can meet you then. See you in a few hours," he said with a sigh.

# CHAPTER 7

*M*ichelle was stretched out on the wheelhouse seats reading emails. This was a busier marina as it was close to the oil refineries and to Caracas. There were more pleasure boats at this marina than the last one. She wondered if the gate lockdown to the dock was any better than at the previous marina. She was also thinking that it would be easy for crooks to approach the boat from the front. She looked at their security software to see the different camera angles for the boat. She checked the settings to make sure that the alarm would go off whenever boats got within forty feet of the front. It made the alarms more sensitive, but it also gave her more warning of unfriendlies.

It was hard to concentrate in the warm, muggy air. She wanted to fall asleep after the lack of sleep the previous night, but it was too hot to sleep. She looked around to see if there were any conversations she might eavesdrop on. She saw men gathered at an outdoor area that looked to be a bar or restaurant. She saw no women inside and wondered if she would stand out. She decided there was no time like the present to try her inadequate acting skills, starting with speaking English only. Maybe everyone would let their guard down and share some secrets. She looked around to see if the boat would be safe if she went beyond the gate and after judging it safe, she walked over to the restaurant.

"Hi! Do you serve food here?" Michelle asked the bartender, doing her best to act like a flaky tourist. She could see they served food as the men were eating.

He gave her a sour look and said, "No English."

Michelle played a game of charades making actions that imitated eating and the man still shook his head. Then she listened as he made derogatory remarks about women in Spanish. Her feelings might be hurt, but she reminded herself she wanted information. She looked blankly at the man and then did another charade about wanting food and a drink. She decided she would dig in her heels and keep up the charades game. She was having a good time wearing him out. You had to get your small pleasures where you could. He was saying increasingly bad things about her, but she kept pointing at food and drink in front of other people. Finally, the proprietor asked one of the men who spoke English to translate for him. Darn, the gig was up.

"Señorita, we serve only men in this restaurant."

"Why? Don't you want to earn more income?" Michelle said. She wasn't going to give up easily.

"The owner orders food to cover the expected customers each day as food is very expensive here. If he feeds you, then one of the men from the docks won't eat. Only men work at the dock."

"Can I have a cocktail or fruit drink? I'm thirsty from our time out on the sea."

Her question was translated to the owner, who cursed a bit more before asking the bilingual patron to tell her that she might have a drink, but he would have to see the money first. American money.

It was interesting that American money was more popular than the Venezuelan currency, which was very volatile and weak. She nodded her agreement and asked for a cola drink. The owner tried to charge $10 but she negotiated him down to $5. She took her drink and sat at the table much to the discomfort of the other patrons. She pulled a book out of her purse and relaxed into her cola and the book. Of course, it was all fake as she was there to listen to them.

There was more grumbling, but eventually the room returned to its conversations. Michelle didn't hear anything of interest and despite the slow sipping of her cola, her drink was nearly finished. It was then she got an alert that someone was near the boat. It was time to leave this inhospitable restaurant.

She walked back to the boat looking at her phone screen to see the location of the problem. Was someone getting too close on land or water? She was relieved to see that Jason was walking toward the boat with an official type. She increased her pace and yelled out his name so he wouldn't be worried about where she was since she was supposed to be aboard the boat.

"I was just having a soda at that unfriendly restaurant," she said pointing to where she had been sitting.

"Was the food good?"

"He wouldn't serve me food. He said he only had enough food for the men he expected to eat at his restaurant today. All I managed to get was a cola for five dollars, but it felt good on my parched throat."

"Okay. This is an official who is inspecting the boat. After he's done, we should have our paperwork finalized for this port."

"Excellent. I'd like to go somewhere to eat. Perhaps the official can recommend somewhere."

"I already took care of getting a few recommendations."

Michelle lowered her voice and asked, "How's the paperwork going? Are they playing games?"

"Actually, this port so far has been better than the last. I think they do business with many more commercial boats and so play fewer games."

The official stepped off the boat, signed something and handed it to Jason, and then left.

"OK, we're good to go in this port for a while. Let's hope we stumble upon new information quickly. Did you discover anything in the restaurant?"

"No. I wasted a lot of time playing charades and pretending not to speak Spanish. I sipped my cola as slowly as I could and read a book while listening to the conversations around me. Mostly, they talked about what a pain I was. The owner gave me the excuse that he only had enough food for the men he expected at the restaurant that day and couldn't feed me. That was fine—I might have gotten food poisoning there."

"Let's lock down the boat and hope we find a more talkative group at one of the restaurants I saw."

"Do we have any protection on the boat? It looks like we could be attacked from land or sea."

"What do you have in mind?"

"Can you operate the drone remotely? We could leave it on top of the boat so it could drop something on anyone approaching our boat. I wish we had a slingshot that could lob smoke bombs at anybody who got too close."

"I need to put the drone out of sight perhaps on the floor of the cockpit, so that it doesn't attract thieves—but yes, I can operate it remotely."

"Awesome. It seems like there is a better lock on the gate down to the dock, but desperate people do desperate things."

Jason unpacked the drone and armed it with smoke bombs, and then they left to eat. Their eyes were on alert for something that had the CIA worried. It was hard to see something unusual in a country filled with chaos.

"This is an odd group of homeless people here," Michelle said.

Jason looked around and agreed, "For a socialist country, they don't have homes, healthcare, or dentistry it appears."

"Yeah, it doesn't look like the homeless of any major American city. We'll have to inquire about that. Have you noticed we're being followed?"

"Yes, though they aren't closing in. Let's step over to the railing and look at the boats and we'll see what they do," Jason said, motioning to a series of docks.

Jason leaned against the rail while Michelle turned sideways to look at Jason, but really to look at the two men following them. They slowed their steps and were talking to each other.

"If they come at us, can we safely heave them over this railing? I don't want to kill them, I just want them to take a dip in the water," Michelle said.

Jason assessed the situation and said, "If you can pitch them over the railing in the space between where we are standing, they should land in the water. If they're not dead center, they'll have a hard landing on a boat."

"Okay, they've decided to take us on. They're approaching and I see a knife in one of their hands—the guy closest to you. I'm going to act scared about the knife, then teleport behind him and toss him over the railing. By that time, I should be able to back you up if you haven't dispatched the guy. Okay, here they come. Turn around."

# CHAPTER 8

$\mathcal{M}$ichelle let out a fake scream, then teleported behind the man and gave him a boost over the railing. The man with the knife kept his arm extended toward Jason but looked sideways at his friend's yell as he went over the railing. Jason took the opportunity to chop the man's forearm and he dropped the knife. Meanwhile, Michelle moved so she was in the position to toss the second man over the railing with Jason's assistance.

They smiled at each other as they heard the second man splash, then Jason held out his hand and they continued their stroll to the restaurant. Just as they turned into the restaurant they both received the alert that someone was near the boat. They sat down and each studied their phone screen. Someone was approaching their boat from the water. It appeared to be another sailboard heading into a close-by slip. They heaved a sigh of relief just about the time a waitress appeared to take their order.

After ordering food, they had minimal conversation between themselves as they tried to listen to what was being said. Fortunately, the service was slow, so they spent an hour listening. Mostly, the workers spoke of bad bosses, but then there was a quiet conversation about a co-worker that died suddenly. Apparently, he was known to try illicit drugs, but the mortician claimed it was the flu that killed him. They used the word *gymson* and Jason and Michelle were soon doing an internet search for the word. They didn't find anything and decided they must've heard the wrong word.

"This is such a poor and chaotic country. How do you think people afford drugs?" Michelle said.

"Maybe it's run by cartels and many people are employed in its creation and production. We're going to have to track the drug down and then maybe you can teleport it to Langley and drop off a sample for Sheila. She can have the powers that be determine what it is."

"Let's head back to the boat. Maybe we'll see one of those homeless people and we can chat them up and see if they can refer us to the distribution system. Have you done any undercover work with the drug cartels?"

"I've been with the agency for over twenty-five years, so I've pretty much been involved in every type of case. I would have to give it some thought, but I'm sure if I scratched my memory, I could find a prior drug case. The CIA rarely gets involved in drug issues as they're not matters of national security. We also don't know if this drug is what the CIA was hearing rumors about. This assignment is very vague, although this isn't my first time with an unclear mission."

"I was on the narcotics squad for a while with the police department. I did the shortest rotation possible as I knew this was an area I didn't want to specialize in. You just see too much human waste and it's depressing as a police officer. I was one of those rare cops who just enjoyed a regular beat—trying to do my part to make the community safer and better."

They were passing the last residence before reaching the marina where their boat was docked. A man exited the building, paused, and looked around in an unfocused manner before collapsing to the pavement.

"I have an urge to go help that man, but we don't want to draw attention to ourselves, and God knows what kind of germs I might catch. Should we stand to the side and see if anyone else comes to his aid? I don't even know what the emergency code is for Venezuela so that we might get an ambulance here," Michelle said.

"I have to agree with you there. The last thing we want is to come to anybody's notice. However, I don't want to be perceived as not caring or being neglectful. Let's step around the corner of this building so we're no longer in that man's line of sight and we'll see if he gets any aid."

The man had not moved since he landed on the pavement. Michelle wondered if the man was dead or had hit his head hard when he landed on the ground. They had been watching for about two minutes when a woman exited the building and whaled in Spanish about the man. She knelt on her knees, pounded on his chest, and had tears streaming down her face.

"Is she going to call emergency services?" Michelle asked.

"She probably doesn't have a cell phone. We either ask someone else to make the call or run back inside and call from a landline. At this point, it's too late. He's been down and unmoving for at least three minutes. Even though he is young, I suspect it's a drug overdose that won't be overcome by someone doing CPR. I wonder if emergency services carry Narcan in this country? I think we've read about complaints by municipalities about the cost of Narcan so I can't imagine this country affording it, but maybe they get a break from the drug manufacturers."

"Not to be insensitive, but I'd love to go over and talk to her. Do you think we could come back tomorrow and ask questions?"

"Someone's going to have to get the body off the pavement. He's going to need to be buried or cremated. He can't just be left there. I wonder who will help move the body. Perhaps we should step in with a cell phone and ask her if she wants anyone called. That will help her and perhaps open the door for us to have a conversation with her about the man's apparent demise."

"Good idea, let's run with it."

They walked over to the woman and asked her in English first and then Spanish if she needed help. The woman was so distraught that she couldn't hear what they were saying. So, Michelle held up her phone and pointed to it. That seemed to momentarily create a break in the woman's sobbing. In poor Spanish, she asked the woman if she would like to call for help or an ambulance.

The woman said there was no ambulance available in Venezuela. Still, she wanted to call her sister so Michelle offered to make that call with her cell phone.

Then Jason asked in Spanish what would happen to the man's body?

She replied that she would have to call a mortician to come and fetch him.

"What did he die from?" Jason asked.

The woman gave a long explanation, and Jason and Michelle figured out that the man had been addicted to *gymson*. They looked at each other, not understanding what the word meant. They would have to pass it on to the analysts at the CIA who could probably figure out what it meant. They helped her make a call to her sister and the mortician and stayed with the woman until her sister arrived. They left the woman and her sister and continued their walk toward the boat.

"I'm grateful that no one harassed the boat while we were assisting that woman," Michelle said.

"Me too. Now I hope that headquarters can figure out what the drug might be that is killing all these people in Venezuela."

"What should we do the rest of the day? I don't want to keep leaving the boat for long periods for fear that thieves will ransack it. I can't stand the thought of sitting in bars or restaurants during all our waking hours. I hope Meeks will have something for us on whatever this *gymson* is."

They would make the call as soon as they were on board the boat and had some privacy.

Michelle saw that another boat had docked in the slip next to them while they were gone. She wondered what country they were from. If you lived in Venezuela, you likely didn't have the money for a sailboat as the economy was wrecked. Why would anybody sail to Venezuela unless they were ordered there by some government agency? The pirates were simply too dangerous off the coast for the country to be on anyone's top ten places they should sail to.

Jason powered up the laptop and connected with Langley. He explained the word that they had been unable to find in a Google search and the analyst planned to run the term down. No one had heard of an illicit product called *gymson*. They decided they would play with multiple combinations of letters to create the word that sounded like *gymson*. Michelle was tempted to ask if any Iranian ships were lost in the Bermuda triangle, but she decided to keep her mouth shut as that was likely information on a need-to-know basis that Sheila wouldn't share in front of the analysts.

"You gave us a vague assignment to find out what was going on in Venezuela. Do you know if it could be a new drug, something about the military here, or a political coup? It's hard to be in a country where we're not welcome and is full of criminals. It seems like half of the people here are bad actors. There are so many trees in the way it's hard to see the forest," Michelle said.

Jason smiled at her words, "Sheila, as you can tell, my partner doesn't like uncertainties, but I'm trying to change her ways. This is one of many vague assignments I've had from the agency, so I'm good. However, it would be good to know what the intel was that got us sent here, as I do have to agree with Michelle that there are so many bad actors here, it is hard to see the forest for the trees in the way."

They both heard Sheila sigh. "We heard rumors of unrest in Venezuela. We don't know if it's due to the economy, the government, or anything else. Now that we know that they're not partnering with Iran, we've let out a sigh of relief. Especially as we received word that Iran recently lost three ships in a tropical storm. They must not have been well-trained sailors.

"If you have the opportunity to get a sample of that drug, please send it to Langley and we'll see what it's all about. We're losing too many Americans as it is to Fentanyl-laced illicit drugs without a new drug being introduced into our market. I'm sure the DEA would like to know more about this so when it hits our shores, we'll know what we're looking at and the damage it's going to cause to our public. As vague as this assignment is, keep at it. Who knows, we may find out that their crap government is hoping to fix the economy by wrecking the rest of the world with a new illicit drug."

The analyst who had been in the room with Sheila and typing away furiously at her computer while they talked broke into the conversation. "There's a plant called *Jimson* that has some dangerous qualities about it. Google it. It's close enough phonetically that it might be the word you heard. See if you can verify that. From what I've read, if jimson was combined with fentanyl, we would see our citizens dying in huge quantities and Narcan wouldn't fix it."

They ended the call, and Michelle and Jason went to work reading about jimson. Michelle said, "I'd love to show the woman who was crying over that man the word *jimson* on a piece of paper and have her verify that this is what she was talking about. Do you think we could find her again and ask that question?"

"As bold a suggestion as yours is, I don't think it would work in this country. Remember that Venezuelans live in chaos and are suspicious of anybody who might make their life worse than it already is. Let's strategize on a different way to ask the same question."

"You're right, of course. It seems like we're finding some small clues that may or may not be significant at this point. Perhaps we remain here for a few days to watch and listen and then circle back to the woman in time to see what she has to say."

"I like that idea. Right now, let's give some thought to defending this boat while we're away. As you said, there are many criminals here and if we want to watch and listen to the public, we need to do it away from the boat. I'd like to get a second drone and some more batteries. Maybe our technical department could think of some more things to drop from the drone or fire from this boat. I'm going to email Sheila now and then maybe you can do a few runs and pick stuff up and bring it back. We'll spend the afternoon on the boat gathering supplies to fortify it," Jason said.

"While I'm gathering supplies, I'll bring back some groceries as well. Make me a list of what we need. In fact, I'll get the groceries first."

Just as planned, Michelle restocked their supplies on the boat. Jason thought that having a partner with Michelle's teleport skill made missions so much easier and safer when you could gather supplies from the field. The technology department developed some battery-operated mousetrap-size catapults that would be mounted around the boat edge. They would be used to launch smoke bombs at anyone who approached looking dubious. The smoke bombs floated on the water so even if they missed an incoming boat or jet ski, there would still be sufficient smoke to protect the boat. Reloaded with supplies, they set off at the dinner hour to find a new place to eavesdrop.

After they were seated, Michelle asked, "Do you think that the men who followed us earlier in the day were doing so because we looked like we had something to steal, or were they following us for a different reason?"

"Despite our trying to fit in here, we don't look like Venezuelans. We've had excellent dental care our entire life and haven't had to perform backbreaking work to earn a minimum wage. I read somewhere that the monthly wage in this country is equal to about four American dollars. That's just inconceivable to me to survive on, which is why you have so many criminals in this country--they're just trying to feed their families."

"You sound fairly sympathetic to the people we tossed in the water. They broke the law by pulling a knife on us. They could've killed us if we weren't so good at self-defense."

"I don't know how I would behave if I lived in this country and had a family to feed. I'd like to think that I would leave and try to establish a life elsewhere. However, if I had a huge family here with both the elderly and the young who needed supporting, I might turn to a life of crime to support them," Jason said.

"This is a depressing conversation. I'll be happy to finish this mission, but you're right. If I saw my son and daughter struggling in this country, I don't know if I would leave for the unknown and potential income or stay here and turn into a thief to feed them."

"Let's listen in to see what we can hear. Perhaps we'll learn all we need to learn tonight and be able to sail back to Curaçao tomorrow."

"Yeah right. Even I am not that much of an optimist. If we do find there's a new drug here that has great potential to harm the United States, we'll probably have to figure out where it's manu-factured and try to do something about that. That's my excuse for bringing back a couple of bags of candy. We're going to be here for the long run."

Jason just smiled and they began to concentrate on the conver-sations around them in Spanish. At one point, Michelle noticed that Jason hit the record button on his cell phone and moved it to the edge of the table presumably to catch the conversation behind him. She wondered what he heard. She said something to him briefly so that it looked like they were in conversation, but then she went back to listening to what she could hear around her, and as far she could tell there was nothing of significance. She under-stood about eighty percent of what was said in Spanish, but it still required a lot of concentration on her part. After an hour or so, she could feel a headache coming on from the effort of concentration.

"I'd love to get some fresh air and then go to another place and listen to the conversations. I'm getting a headache from concentrating on what people say and some fresh air would clear out the cobwebs in my brain."

"I know what you mean, I'm working on my own headache in part from the cigarette smoke here. I hate that the government is not looking over its own citizens and banning smoking indoors, but I guess they have far bigger problems to worry about. Let's go."

They looked for a new place to go and have a drink. They had dinner at the last restaurant and were now looking for a bar that would be a safe place for two Americans to hang out. In many parts of the world, port bars and restaurants were not the safest places and were prone to fights breaking out between customers. On top of that was the general hatred that the Venezuelan government had toward America, and that only added to the tension of any place they visited. When push came to shove, they would display passports from Panama, so at the very least they look like expatriate Americans.

The bar they selected was a complete bust. When the two of them appeared at the bar, it was like the Red Sea parting. People who had been close to them as they approached the counter magically moved away so they were not within earshot of anything being said. They gave up and went home to the boat.

"Do you think it would help if we wore Venezuelan sports star shirts? There's a bunch of players from Venezuela who play for Major League baseball teams."

"That's a great idea, Michelle," Jason said looking at his watch. "You'll have to go to a store on the West Coast as the East Coast stores are already closed. I would think if you hit a major mall in

Los Angeles, you would find a store inside that sold Dodgers or Angels gear. I'll do a quick Google search and find some names."

It had been a quiet evening for the boat with no attacks. They went below and developed a list of names and stores that Michelle could visit in the next hour.

"I think I'll stop off at the hotel suite in Curaçao on the way here for a decent shower. Be back soon. Call me if you need help."

Jason looked up and watched her disappear in front of him, wishing he could stop at a hotel for a shower of endless water. Actually, he would be a very happy human being if he could teleport as Michelle did.

# CHAPTER 9

*A*fter a quiet night aboard the boat, they were sitting on the deck enjoying coffee and breakfast and watching the marina. It was a little busier than the previous marina they had stayed at but still quiet compared to an American marina. Michelle had managed to find two baseball shirts for both of them with different names of Venezuelan players on the back. They brushed up on the players' skills and statistics in hopes that they might use that as a way into conversations at restaurants and bars.

"Where are the other boats from in this marina?" Michelle asked.

"Hard to say. All of the boats are flying the Venezuelan flag out of respect and not wanting to agitate the government officials we have to deal with. With only five or six other boats here, we should just go make friends and see if we hear anything from them."

"We need to be careful there as I'm sailboat stupid. Why don't we fill out a back story first that says how long we've been sailing and what other ports or countries we visited recently? It wouldn't do if we told two different stories."

"True. I'll write something down for us to memorize." True to his word, Jason had a story which they both memorized; twenty minutes later then they set off to see if they could make friends on any of the other boats.

It turned out to be a bad idea. Some of the boats were truly Venezuelan and wanted nothing to do with the Americans. One was empty, its owners elsewhere. One boat was from Panama and appeared to have been confiscated by the harbor police. The final few boats had been successfully attacked by pirates and were scared to meet any strangers.

"Okay, that was a bad idea. It feels like all the happiness has been sucked out of the atmosphere in this country. It's such a shame. I've read a few sailing blogs from twenty or thirty years ago when people were happy to stop by this country, but now it's a wreck."

"So maybe I can convince you to go sailing with me when we return home? You found something enjoyable in some of those sailing blogs that made you want to try going for a sail on my boat in the Chesapeake Bay?"

"Maybe in the summer. It seems too cold there in the winter to be out on the water with a stiff breeze blowing at you. I'm still occasionally getting seasick, but it's a nice weight-loss measure. I'm not prone to snacking when I'm nauseated and that's a good thing."

"There's a bright way to look at it! How about we spend the morning hanging out near where that man died yesterday? We'll see if we can have a conversation with the woman. Do you remember what she looks like?"

"I think so, but I would be the first to admit that her flood of tears changes the way her face looks."

Jason nodded and again they worked out a strategy to question the woman, but in as pleasant a manner as possible in hopes that she wouldn't notice that they were interviewing her.

On their third pass around the block where the building was located, they caught a glimpse of her returning to the building.

Jason called out in Spanish to get her attention. She looked over at the two of them and recognized them from the previous day and stopped to say something. Jason whispered to Michelle to turn on the record feature on her phone. They might need help with the Spanish later.

Speaking in halting Spanish, Jason conveyed their condolences on the man's death and asked her how she was doing. They seem to hit her at the right moment as she unloaded about the misery of the last twenty-four hours. She told them of her woes in planning the funeral, and Michelle was able to ask amid the woman's story if she knew why the man died. Again, they heard the word *jimson* in the flow of her words and so they had an opportune time to question her about what she knew.

After they had an explanation of what was going on, Michelle and Jason knew this was why the CIA sent them to Venezuela. The man who died was her brother. He had addiction problems most of his life and bounced between illicit drugs and alcohol. The brother met a man in a bar who offered him a new substance to try and of course, he did. In the first three weeks or so, her brother was the happiest she'd ever seen him. To talk to him, you wouldn't realize he was on drugs. Then, he changed this week. He didn't feel well, started throwing up. Then he started seeing things yesterday and he ran outside to get away from monsters, saying he couldn't breathe, and then he collapsed and died.

Jason asked the woman if she knew what drug her brother was taking.

She gave two names—*jimson* and *el diablo*. She said that family members called it the devil as it was so addictive and seemed to kill everyone who took it within a month.

Jason and Michelle looked suitably alarmed and asked if he had taken the drug before he ran outside.

The sister said he had felt so bad the last couple of days he hadn't wanted to use the drug. Jason looked at Michelle, clearly suggesting she go search the apartment. She looked at the building but had no idea which apartment housed the brother and sister. Oh well, she would bounce in and out of the rooms until she found something. The building was one story but she couldn't guess the number of apartments. She passed the phone to Jason and said she forgot something and had to go retrieve it. The moment she was beyond the women's line of sight she disappeared inside the building. She was grateful that the woman hadn't exited one of many tall apartment buildings. With this building, she had a fighting chance of finding the right apartment. She thought when she teleported that she would end up in a hallway with entrances to apartments. Instead, and with good fortune, she ended up in a single apartment with the door that the woman had exited from the previous day.

She did a quick search of the small space to make sure she was alone. She tried to figure out where the brother's stuff was. There was one bedroom and it look like it belonged to the woman. So perhaps the man slept on the sofa. She searched around the sofa cushions and looked in drawers before moving on to the kitchen. She saw no evidence of the illicit drug. She wondered where else she could look? Was it something stored in a refrigerator? She remembered hearing about routine blackouts as the country lost power. She wondered if the refrigerator contained much of anything given that it might spoil with the blackout. She opened the door and there was no lighting inside. Fortunately, there was a fair amount of sunlight coming in through the window and she could see the contents of the refrigerator. There was one unlabeled bottle that she stuffed in her pocket. She quietly shut the refrigerator door just as she heard the front door open. She teleported back to their boat, afraid that she might land on top of Jason or get hit by a car if she went to the front of the building. She put the container in the boat's refrigerator and teleported back to a safe area between the boat and where Jason had been so she could walk back with him. The streets were dangerous, and they shouldn't really be out by themselves. They needed to appear to people to look vulnerable yet ward off any attacks by the Venezuelan criminals. She would've texted him her position or checked with him to see if it was safe to teleport, but she'd left her phone with him still recording the conversation with the distraught woman. She had no way to reach him other than to meet him on the street.

He had barely moved on from the location near the woman's apartment. Michelle was glad to see in the few minutes that she had been gone, no criminals had made a move on him. Soon, she was standing next to him, which made him jump in surprise.

"Did you find anything?"

"I might have. There was a bottle in the refrigerator that was unmarked with some kind of liquid in it. It's sitting in the boat refrigerator at the moment. I just wanted to make sure you got back to the boat safely as the streets are so full of criminals here."

"Poverty will do that to you. I gave the woman all the cash I had in my pocket as I felt so bad for her. I know she won't spend it on drugs. She will probably use it either for the funeral or to pay her rent or buy food, which is a good use of my spare cash."

"You're a very kind man, Jason. Thank you for helping her. As soon as we return to the boat, I'll transport the bottle to Sheila's office. Do you have my cell phone and is it still recording?"

"Darn, I forgot all about it. It is still recording. I'll give it back to you and see if you can shut it off and maybe erase our conversation."

He handed the phone to her and noticed the sound of a scooter growing louder. He looked over Michelle's shoulder and decided that the scooter must be heading toward them. Apparently, they were perceived as good robbery material. This was getting very tiresome.

Michelle had also noticed the motorcycle and was looking around for a safe place.

"Let's hustle and step up on that stoop over there and plan to fight the guy off if he continues to come our way. A few stray kicks from the doorway should put the motorcyclist out of commission."

Jason nodded and they both stepped up onto the narrow stoop. The motorcyclist was prevented from running them down. Now they just needed to knock him or her down. Michelle began a countdown as the bike loomed closer. When she hit the number three, they both let out quick jabs with their legs, which knocked the rider off the bike. They thought about going to his aid or seeing who was behind the helmet, but Michelle was tired of these idiot criminals and she just wanted to walk away, so they did.

"Let's hustle back to the boat before he figures out what happened and comes after us," Jason said.

They took off at a fast pace and were sweating by the time they reached the docks, but there were no additional bad actors. They immediately went to the refrigerator to make sure the product was still there even though no boat alarm sounded.

"It might be mango juice for all I know. I would sniff it but I don't know what jimson smells like, and whoever is manufacturing it could be adding flavor. Did the woman ever say whether this came in pill form or powder or liquid?"

"She didn't say, and I thought it would be awfully suspicious of me to ask that question."

"If I understood the apartment correctly, he slept in the living room and she had a bedroom. I checked many drawers and the sofa cushions thinking he might have dumped something there. Then I looked at the refrigerator and brought this liquid with me just as the woman opened her front door. I wonder if she'll notice that it's missing. I'm sure it has a street value. Perhaps she was hoping to sell it to pay for her brother's funeral."

"I have no idea what she'll do. She hated the drugs that her brother took, but she's also living in deep poverty, and desperate times call for desperate measures. Let's check with Sheila to see if you can take it to Langley right now."

Michelle texted Sheila and waited for a response. Fewer than five people at the CIA knew Michelle's special skill and she wanted to keep it that way. If word ever got out into the world at large about her skill set, she would end up as a target from all of America's enemies.

Sheila wasn't in her office. She had had to go to DC for a meeting. She pulled over and texted a picture of where her car was so that Michelle could teleport to her location. Seconds later Michelle disappeared from Jason's vision. About ten minutes later she was back in the boat cabin.

"She was going to give it to the lab to analyze. Now we need to figure out where this jimson comes from and what exactly they're mixing it with. How do we find a dealer for this drug?"

"I don't know if the woman knows who the dealer is since her brother was using, not her. She might be willing to talk to us tomorrow if she knows there's more money that we can throw her way. I'm afraid to ask the random street thug where I might find a supply. Either they'll think I have a lot of cash and make me a target, or they'll turn me over to the government claiming I'm using drugs."

"We could also find other users and put them under surveillance. Or maybe once we get the analysis back from the CIA that will clue us in to where we might look for the distribution system. I wonder if the DEA could lend us any assistance since we're both newbies at following a drug supply chain?"

"When you were a cop, did you routinely call the DEA or FBI for assistance on cases?"

"No. I see your point. That was a bad suggestion on my part," Michelle said.

"We have this boat slip rented for a week. Given all the empty slips around here, I'm sure I could extend it for another week and claim that we're waiting on a boat part—that would give us an excuse to hang around this hostile country. Of course, I'd rather solve the case today and get the hell out of here."

"I agree with you. I'm hopeful that the CIA will get back to us today on what was in that liquid. If they say it's just some kind of fruit juice, we'll have to figure out a different strategy for finding a supply of the drug. I think we should stay aboard this boat until at least dinner time. I wouldn't want rumors to get started that around the port is an American couple who toss criminals into the water or otherwise disable them. I don't know how the police work in this country, but I do know we don't want to gain their attention."

"I agree with you. I've been on many assignments in hostile countries. As painful as it is to waste time by lying low, sometimes you have to do that to survive. We can play a game of cards or find some maintenance to do aboard the boat."

"Maintenance? We need to sail this boat out of Venezuelan waters at some point. You have my vote that we work on maintenance. What can I help with?"

"We'll check the bilge, batteries, raw water flows, the generator, and our anchor chain."

"I don't know the process for doing any of that, but give me a few instructions and I'm game."

They spent the rest of the afternoon working on the sailboat. It was good for the boat and a perfect activity for their cover of being sailors. They were a sweaty, dirty mess after their work, so Michelle teleported back to Curaçao for a real shower, while Jason used the boat's shower. Just as she returned, they received the communication from Sheila that they had results on the bottle of liquid that Michelle had taken from the woman's refrigerator. A few minutes later they were scheduled to be on a secure phone call to discuss the substance.

# CHAPTER 10

"*I*t must be an interesting substance for us to have a scheduled call versus just a text describing a bottle of fruit juice," Michelle said.

"Indeed. It was a good decision on your part to pull the bottle out of the refrigerator. I'm not sure I would've been immediately suspicious with an unlabeled bottle."

Their phone call connected, and they heard Sheila's voice.

"The analysis came back and according to our chemists and a physician, this is a very dangerous substance. It plays with the brain chemistry while destroying the liver and kidneys. It would kill most people with heart issues of a fast beat and high blood pressure. If a user survives that, they still might die by overheating. To make matters worse, it's been mixed with a tasty fruit juice. Since the juice is so tasty, the user may drink more than they should," Sheila said. "I'm just reading off notes from our experts here."

"That sounds like what the woman we spoke with this morning described. That was the recording we sent you that is in Spanish. Michelle and I understand Spanish passably, but it wouldn't hurt to have someone listen to it who is fluent in Spanish and gets the nuances of the language," Jason said.

"I already did that. We also shared that with the physician, and he said it perfectly matched what they know about jimson and fentanyl. He had a long explanation about brain chemistry and addiction. The question is, what is going on with this drug? Is there a government plan to infiltrate the United States and start a worse drug addiction problem than we already have; or is this run by some kind of cartel in Venezuela outside of the government that simply wants to make money? I don't know which scenario is worse. Given the form this drug combination comes in, it would be hard to detect at the border. We need to know how they're manufacturing it. Are they drying the jimson weed and adding fentanyl to it and then adding the powder to a particular fruit drink? Or are they selling it in powder form with instructions to mix it with the fruit juice? It's too bad we can't get our hands on a dead body in Venezuela so we can better understand how it's distributed and used," Sheila said.

"We talked about trying to find the distribution system for this drug. As you know, we are hearing people talk about it in bars and restaurants here. We were planning to head out for dinner in the hope that would give us new information. However, is this the issue that the CIA wanted us to chase in Venezuela? We haven't seen anything else that has grabbed our attention, but does the agency usually get involved with new designer drugs headed to the United States?" Michelle asked.

"That is not usually our mission. However, if the Nicholas Maduro Administration can prop itself up by setting up a drug cartel with profits from the United States, then we would have a strong role in preventing that. There's a humanitarian crisis due to the economy in Venezuela, but we don't want that fixed by drug sales," Sheila said.

"So, what are the next steps that the agency wants us to take? I don't like this country and would like to get out of it as soon as possible. It feels like we're two good guys taking on an entire corrupt nation," Michelle said.

"We need to stop this drug from arriving in the United States, and we have no evidence that it has reached our shores yet. Jimson is known as an herbal remedy in parts of West Virginia and teenagers have emergency room visits due to hallucinations. They are chewing on the white flowers. However, our chemists said this was a more concentrated potion, and the addition of fentanyl makes it so much worse. So, we need to find the manufacturing and distribution process as that will probably inform our next steps."

"I understand that, Sheila, but how do we find where these drug substances are being manufactured? Any suggestions on where we should look? Neither Jason nor I particularly have experience with the drug world."

"Neither do I. I have all kinds of expertise on idiots around the world who mean harm to America, but drugs as a means of destroying America is completely new to me and the CIA. I have a meeting later with some folks over at the DEA. As much as I hate involving another agency, we need to do that in this case so that we can get you out of there as soon as possible."

Michelle looked over at Jason to see if he had a sense of where they were going next, but he just shrugged.

"Do you have any sense of where the jimson weed is grown in Venezuela? Maybe that might help us find the manufacturing if we knew where it was grown," Michelle asked.

"Sorry, it grows in most temperate zones in the world. It is toxic to animals that eat it, so I wouldn't think it would be near any cattle ranches, but that is about all I can do to narrow it down."

"That's not good. If it is so prevalent everywhere, how can we permanently destroy it?" Jason asked.

"We can't, but someone is growing it in nitrogen-rich soil to increase the concentration of alkaloids which is what causes hallucinations, and combined with synthetic fentanyl, it seems like you're looking for a greenhouse and a chemistry laboratory," Sheila said.

"I don't understand the juice. I wonder if it comes with instructions to mix it with fruit juice? Given the unequal refrigeration here because there are blackouts, you would think you might lose your expensive illicit drug if the power goes out and the fruit juice goes bad because it's not refrigerated. Maybe we can circle back to that woman in a day or two and ask her about how her brother took the drug? She doesn't know that I stole the bottle of fruit juice out of her refrigerator. I'm not even sure in her state of grieving if she would notice that it was gone."

"She was grateful for the cash I gave her. Perhaps if the agency replenishes my cash supply, I can pass some more money over to her. I just need to figure out how we can do this on an accidental basis as I don't want her suspicions to be raised."

"Michelle can stop by for some more cash. This woman seems to be our closest link to this drug, so anything we can do to help her helps us."

They ended the call shortly and Jason and Michelle discussed where they would go eat that evening. Michelle made a quick stop at Sheila's office to pick up more cash for Jason and then they set off toward the restaurants in the port area.

"I wonder if we should focus on another area to dine. Our reason for choosing to dine at the port was we thought this was where the activity was, but if we're chasing an illicit drug perhaps the port isn't the right place to eavesdrop," Jason said.

"If the side effects are as bad as they sound, perhaps we should hang out near a major hospital here as surely some victims are making it to the hospital?"

"Maybe we should strategize on where the drug users might be and get some listening devices from Langley to place in those locations. Langley has better Spanish listeners than you and I. They might hear something relevant."

"That's not a bad suggestion. Why don't you text Sheila once we get seated at a restaurant and I'll go retrieve the devices? I would suggest that we bug that woman's house, but we don't even know if she knows who the dealer is who sold her brother the drug. Hopefully, after Sheila meets with the DEA, they'll have some expert advice on where we can find drug dealers in Venezuela."

"Did you stay in contact with anybody from your old police department? Could you contact someone there who could give us the skinny on drug dealer behavior?"

"That's an interesting idea. Let me log in to their website and see if I recognize any names on the narcotics squad. They know I work for the CIA now, so they'll know this is a professional question on my part. They might be surprised to find that I'm in Venezuela, but I will mention that as it may have bearing on what they tell me. I would think that drug dealers in San Jose who offer designer drugs to the Silicon Valley elite behave a little differently than someone from the drug cartel in Mexico, but what do I know?"

Another group of thugs followed them as they made their way from the boat to the restaurant; they were able to dispatch them pretty quickly. They were soon seated at a restaurant and Jason began texting their thoughts to Sheila while Michelle looked up her old department to see if she knew anyone on the narcotics squad. She found a name she knew and sent off an email. They heard no interesting conversations in this restaurant and discussed going to a nearby bar to see what they could pick up.

"I think I'd rather go back to the boat. The likelihood of our finding new information by randomly picking a port bar seems like long odds. Let's surf the Internet and see what we can come up with our own."

"Okay. We do have a bottle of wine back on the boat, and you're right about doing some research on drug dealers since we know so little ourselves. So, here's the question of the evening, will we have one or two groups of folks to deal with on our way back to the boat?" Jason asked.

"My money is on two as it's dark now, so we look more vulnerable. It's a good thing that these guys aren't stealthy in their approach. It makes them easier to take them down."

They were both wrong as no one bothered them on their way back to the boat.

"Maybe we have a reputation among the local thug community of being impossible to rob. If that's the case, I'm thrilled," Michelle said.

"I agree. We can defend well against fists and knives, but multiple guns become a little harder."

"Perhaps we should start carrying pepper spray? Is it legal in this country?"

"I don't know. One more thing to add to our research list. The last thing we want to do is give Venezuelan authorities a reason to pay attention to us or arrest us."

They stepped aboard their boat and went below to grab their laptops a bottle of wine and glasses. Soon they were sipping a nice red blend to the sound of keyboards clicking. After two glasses of wine apiece and nearly an hour of research, they were ready to discuss their findings.

"I sent an email to an old colleague who was on the narc squad. He actually replied to my question after about thirty minutes. He gave me a list of questions to think about in our search for the manufacturing source. He also added that if someone let that drug loose in America, we would see a mounting death rate. People with addictions would be unable to resist this powerful combination in the Venezuelan drug. What did you find?"

"Probably the same as your colleague told you. Apparently, you can find clusters of illicit drug use in different places. At your lowest tier are the homeless, who will spend any dime they have on street drugs and alcohol. There's another cluster around women in prostitution or human trafficking where drugs are used to dull the reality that they're living in. Finally, there's a third area where the middle and upper class go to buy drugs. Often this is in bars or nightclubs. With the damaged economy of Venezuela, I would think our best bet would be to find some bars or nightclubs where the few people who have money hang out. For that, I think we have to go inland to Caracas as it's reputed to have food and electricity when most of the rest of the country does not. So, if you're wealthy, I would think you would hang out there. Also, there are probably a few wealthy people behind the scenes who pull the strings on the current government. They would be located near the capital so they could be ready with influence at any moment."

"I agree. Should we pay somebody to stay on the boat and keep it safe? Take a taxi to Caracas and stay in one of the few nice hotels? I understand the financial district is relatively safe and it's where the upscale restaurants and nightclubs are located."

"That sounds like a plan. We'll stay here overnight then contact someone at the marina office to find us someone to stay on the boat. I have a credit card that matches my Panamanian passport, and I won't be heartbroken over getting regular showers in a luxury hotel. Let's drop Sheila a note about our new direction. I think it's a good one."

They got an email from Sheila that she agreed with their strategy. Michelle teleported home to both her house and Jason's to collect clothes that they would need to hang out in an upscale nightclub. They hadn't brought such clothing aboard the sailboat.

They made plans the next morning for someone to stay aboard the boat. As Michelle had recently stocked the boat with groceries, they suspected that their boat sitter would eat well until their return.

# CHAPTER 11

hey headed into Caracas mid-afternoon to match the time they could check into a hotel. It was a major American brand hotel and surprisingly was surviving in the chaotic economy. As soon as they reached their suite, Jason headed for the shower. The suite featured two bedrooms, a living room, and a bathroom. While Jason was showering, Michelle surveyed the room for hidden cameras or listening devices. She found a camera in a smoke detector and covered the lens with a Band-Aid.

Before heading to the shower herself, she explained what she found in a whisper to Jason and then caught sight of the sliding glass doors behind some drapes leading to a balcony and noted that she hadn't checked there. She headed into the bathroom herself while Jason went to work. He hit pay dirt with listening devices around the balcony, but no cameras. He came back inside and turned the television on and selected a random station. He rearranged the furniture so that the TV was near the balcony and then turned up the volume.

Michelle noted the furniture rearranging and volume coming from the television and figured out what was going on. They moved the furniture away from the TV and closer to the door, figuring their conversation was secure.

"Did you check the door from the hallway or bathroom? I didn't," Michelle whispered.

Jason shook his head and pulled out the scanner to do so. The hallway had a camera on their door and listening bugs randomly in the hallway. He noted those but knew not to disable them. The bathroom was fortunately clear. They sat in the living room conversing in low voices.

"I can't imagine they have the resources to constantly listen to guests all day. Perhaps they turn on the devices at the government's direction when they are suspicious of people," Jason said.

"I agree. We have about four restaurants and nightclubs to target tonight. Perhaps I should go talk to the concierge about additional nightclubs."

"Do they have a concierge here?"

"Good question. They must have something given the price they charge for the rooms here. I was thinking of scheduling us on one of those walking tours so we can experience Venezuelan food up close and personal. That would give us an excuse to move around here, and we could see if there are any other locations where we might find drugs."

"Good idea. See what you can come up with. Why don't you explore that right now? It might change our plans for tonight."

"Okay, be right back."

She asked in halting Spanish for directions to the concierge. She was informed they didn't have one, but an assistant manager could help with any inquiries. She was shown to the man's office and Michelle asked questions about what to see in Caracas, where to eat, nightclub suggestions, and walking tours.

"We researched the city and have some ideas of what we want to see, but it's better to speak to an expert," she told the man hoping to puff up his ego.

It worked like a charm and thirty minutes later she walked out with a wide range of suggestions and a reservation for a private walking tour the next day. Hopefully, they would find a drug dealer within the next twenty-four hours.

Jason and Michelle had another call with Langley, which had more information on the drug. It seemed that some plant expert determined it was a special variety of jimson that had been grafted to create an unusual concentration of alkaloids. They figured out the plant was genetically altered rather than grown in nitrogen-rich soil.

After reporting all of the new information, Sheila summarized, "So, the good news there is it's a special crop that we can target once we find its location. Some botanist is working on a poison to destroy it completely, and depending on where the crop is, we may need you to play a role in that."

"I have a drone here and Michelle can fetch additional drones. Find an application that we can disperse at night with a drone."

"Yes, that is our intent. Not only do we need to kill the plant, but we also have to sterilize it so its dying spores can't move on and propagate. Those are the botanist's words, not mine."

"You're putting a pretty big assignment on our shoulders," Michelle said, thinking about all they didn't know about what was going on in this country.

"Yeah, well suck it up Buttercup. You saved the world last month; now we just want you to save the United States. This should be a slam dunk."

"Ha!" Michelle replied. "That was easier than this assignment. There I didn't have to spend days in a hostile country worried about my partner. I could just disappear when the going got tough."

"Yeah, we'll find the distribution system quickly and the plant source and we'll have you sailing back to a vacation in Curaçao. Michelle, look at the bright side, I'm not asking you to destroy the entire Colombian cocaine industry."

They both heard a snort come from Michelle.

"Did the DEA have anything to say about the distribution process in Venezuela?" Jason asked.

"She filled me in on a lot of information about drugs in Venezuela. Some experts think that twenty percent of the world's cocaine coming from Colombia travels through Venezuela and is distributed mostly through the Caribbean to the rest of the world. Venezuela has also started distributing to the Middle East through its partnership with Iran. Two of Nicholas Maduro's nephews were arrested and convicted for their involvement in the cocaine trade via Miami in New York City. We believe the government is heavily involved in drug distribution as a source of income. Several of the Mexican cartels and one of the Colombian cartels have representatives and connections in Venezuela. There is some use by Venezuelans of illegal drugs, but with ninety percent of the people living in poverty, it's simply not affordable."

"So this is going to be like looking for a needle in a haystack. We have to find that rare, rich, corrupt Venezuelan who can afford to use illicit drugs," Jason said.

"How did the guy who died in front of us afford a brand-new designer drug? Do you think Venezuela is testing the drug out on its own population? I know the idea sounds absurd, but I find much about this country absurd," Michelle said.

There was silence over the phone call as everyone pondered Michelle's theory.

"Maybe. . . . He has done so many other awful things to his country, what's the death of a few of his countrymen as they test out a new drug? Here's a question for your victim's sister—was her brother paid to try the drug?" Sheila suggested.

"Unless we take a taxi back to the coast, we're too far away to run into her now. That question will have to wait a few days until after we've returned to the sailboat. We can safeguard the sailboat and search for new information. We need to return it or park it somewhere safer than Venezuela," Jason said. "That delay is probably a good thing as we don't want to make her suspicious by being around her too much."

"Let's hope you learn something tonight hanging around the rich and ridiculous of Venezuela. You really are in grave danger in that country and Michelle's right to be worried." With that promising bit of sage advice from Sheila Meeks, their call ended.

"She's right, Jason. If we get arrested, I can disappear before they can handcuff me. You, however, are in grave danger as Sheila said."

"I've been in tight spots before. Really, you're my secret weapon. Knowing that you could appear in my jail cell and hand me all kinds of weapons makes me a lot less anxious. Furthermore, knowing that you could be by my side as we fight our way out reduces my concern about the situation."

Michelle gave him a pained look and instead said, "I'm going to change for dinner and whatever else the night brings."

Jason knew he needed a lot less time than his partner to get ready for an evening in Caracas. He had a suit that would take him all of five minutes to put on. He understood Michelle's concern, but he also knew that she had performed countless hostage rescues for the CIA before they became partners. She could rescue him also.

He thought some more about the question as to whether Venezuela would test a new drug on its own citizens. The two places they had heard about the jimson were in a port bar and outside a sad apartment building. Maybe they were targeting the wrong location tonight. Surely if the rich and famous knew that you would have an incredible high for three weeks and then your organs would start shutting down and you would hallucinate, would anybody willingly take that drug with advance notice of its side effects? If the rich and politically elite were in on a government conspiracy to create and sell this new drug to help their coffers, then there wouldn't likely be dealing going on tonight. He didn't know what to think. It sounded like the new drug was highly addictive and potentially you were hooked after one swallow of it, and you couldn't stop the desire for more until your body was destroyed. It sure would be a nice way to get rid of your enemies. They would enjoy your concoction until it was too late.

About ten minutes sooner than Jason expected, Michelle came out of her bedroom all set to light the town on fire. She looked gorgeous. She had brunette hair with streaks of sunlight in it. The black dress accentuated curves, and you would never know at first glance that she was in her fifties and a mother of two adult children. You also wouldn't take her to be a kick-ass cop or CIA case officer. Michelle canceled all of your preconceived notions about people in all of those categories.

"You look gorgeous and very un-CIA-like. It will take me five minutes to change. I didn't think you'd be so fast."

"Thanks for the compliment, but it didn't take me too long to get dressed. Just a little makeup and a few curls in my hair and I'm good to go. As always, I'm looking to be your brainless sidekick in hopes that I will lower the guard of people I come into contact with."

"You've got the look to do that tonight."

Jason was back as he expected in just under five minutes.

"You don't look so bad yourself! You sort of have that secret agent look like you're the next actor for a James Bond movie."

"We sure are full of compliments for each other tonight, and that's before we've had any alcohol. Let's go, partner."

Before they left, they booby-trapped the room in case someone tried to get in. They also found a great place to hide their technology. They left a decoy laptop sitting on the desk and put the real one in between a stack of towels in the bathroom. They also hid a few things in the oven and on top of a closet that didn't quite go to the ceiling. There was just enough space to stash a laptop. To see it, someone would have to stand on top of a chair and shine a flashlight at it. They held hands as they headed down the hallway to the elevator. They needed to look like a couple.

They smiled at each other in the elevator but didn't say anything assuming that it too was bugged and perhaps had cameras.

A taxi took them to a prominent Venezuelan restaurant where they had an enjoyable meal and most of a bottle of wine. After lingering over the wine, they walked a few blocks to a nightclub that they had both researched and was confirmed by the hotel's assistant manager as being a happening place. The club played Latin music and a few couples were on the dance floor. They both got seltzer water with a twist of lime. That way they would look like they were drinking cocktails, but they weren't adding alcohol to the wine they had already consumed. They huddled close in a corner whispering to each other and very much looking like lovers out on a date. Of course, they were using the huddle to tell each other what they saw as they glanced around the room.

Michelle's cop eyes quickly picked up who was drunk and who was in control. She watched for any passes of cash between people but saw nothing. Her eyes returned to Jason, and she asked him if he'd seen anything, and he said no. Maybe they would stay another hour and then call it a night. It seemed like this was going to be a bust, but they had to try. After spending the hour, they were going deaf from the loud music and were noticing nothing of significance. They looked out for girls who might be victims of human trafficking but saw none that fit their stereotype. They called it a night and headed back to the hotel again in a taxi, in part because Michelle was in high heels and the street pavement was uneven. They made it home without incident and checked the traps they had laid in the hotel room. It appeared that no one had been there in their absence.

After turning the TV on again, they sat next to each other on the sofa and talked about what they had seen.

"It wasn't that busy tonight. I've never been in a Venezuelan nightclub before, so maybe they're always like that as compared to a big American city," Jason said.

"I'm back to wondering if we're targeting the wrong population for the use of this drug. Did we hear or see anything about jimson weed in our previous port?"

"That was a poorer marina than the one we're currently in and I don't recall hearing any mention of the jimson weed. I'm starting to think it must be manufactured somewhere in this region and that your offhand comment about Venezuela trying it on its own citizens might be closer to the truth than we think."

"I don't think I saw anybody dealing any illegal substance in that nightclub. Either my eyesight is terrible, or they had magicians trading cash for drugs. Perhaps everyone has a stash of drugs already at home and they used it before coming to the nightclub. I don't know how the wealthy act in this country when there is such intense poverty everywhere, and they don't seem to arrest people for illicit drugs from what I read."

"Should we bail and return to the sailboat?" Jason asked.

"Good question. We don't want to come to anybody's attention, but we are already on someone's radar as we're staying in an American-owned hotel. I think we should stay at least one more night because we have the tour tomorrow and we'll see if we can pick up any street gossip. If we find nothing, then we can leave the following morning. How's that sound for a plan?"

Jason nodded and they soon parted to their respective bedrooms to get a good night's sleep in the luxury of a bed in an air-conditioned hotel room.

# CHAPTER 12

$\mathcal{T}$he city food tour was wonderful. They learned a lot about Venezuelan culture, customs, and food. There were a few brief moments that Michelle forgot she was on a dangerous CIA operation looking for drug lords as their tour guide was so knowledgeable and enjoyable to be around. They ate at a vintage Venezuelan restaurant and enjoyed the wide variety of tastes of what they were served. As they were walking down one street, Jason said, "Wait here," and he took off after someone, hoping to talk to them. He quickly disappeared.

Michelle saw a wall that she and the tour guide could sit on while they waited for Jason to return. Michelle hadn't seen anything when he took off, so she didn't know what he was chasing. She focused on the tour guide and asked her many questions that kept them occupied until Jason returned.

"You took off so fast that I didn't see what you were chasing. I'm glad to know you're okay."

"You know when you get a glimpse of someone that you think you know, but they're not in the right place? I had to find the person to confirm what my eyes thought they saw. I was wrong I didn't know the person. What did I miss?"

So, Jason had seen something related to their case? She wondered what that was. It was obviously something he couldn't say in front of their tour guide and whatever he saw had no time urgency as he could wait to tell her the real story.

The tour lasted for another hour. It really was an informative cover for checking things out. Michelle knew she would never visit Caracas as a tourist, so at least she saw the high points in the history of the city and had a real sense of the food culture. It had to be the only positive that came out of this mission so far. They gave the tour guide a very generous tip both because her tour was excellent and because they wanted to help the everyday people of Venezuela where they could.

The guide returned them to the hotel; they returned to their suite and turned the TV on for sound cover. Then Jason used the scanner to see if there were any new devices in their room.

"This is not good news," Jason said when the scanner alerted him to new devices.

"Camera or listening device?" Michelle asked.

"Camera."

"Maybe that was the hotel's response to our covering up the camera that was already in the room, but I don't think so. Someone's watching us and that's a bad thing."

"Yes."

"Should we take a taxi to the coast, hop aboard the boat, and leave?" Michelle asked.

"Let me take a look at the recording of the boat cameras. Let's see if any government officials have raided our boat."

He pulled up the security software for the boat and rewound it for the past twenty-four hours. They watched it together and saw three officials board the boat. They didn't find their weapons stash in the bottom of the boat, but they did confiscate the two drones, the sea scooter, and the prop laptop they left behind.

"Is there any drone camera footage of us releasing smoke bombs on the pirate boats?" Michelle asked.

"No. I didn't use the record feature while using the drone mostly because it drains the battery faster. I didn't even think about leaving evidence behind of us taking out Venezuelan pirates."

"Do you think we could return to the boat and sail out of the marina before any government officials noticed?"

"I doubt it, and their police boats are faster than our sailboat. We might make an attempt in the dark with no lights on and no radar beacon. We would be in international waters at twelve miles in less than two hours. Since they're such a corrupt country they would probably ignore international law and still go after us. They could arrest us for not completing the paperwork required to leave the country."

"If we didn't have the radar beacon, would we be able to see obstructions in the water? How would we get out of this marina without hitting something?"

"Packed in with our cachet of weapons are some night vision goggles. We would have to wear those out on the water. You would have to be at the front of the boat looking for obstructions while I steered."

"This sounds like a really flawed escape plan. We're in a slow boat and we don't have the paperwork that the authorities want us to have. Is there any incoming weather that might make our escape easier?" Michelle asked.

"Let me look," Jason said and there was silence. "We might be in luck. There's a rainstorm scheduled for tomorrow night. It will be windy with it which means you'll likely be seasick."

"Better to be seasick than worried about you in jail. If we get arrested before we get out of this hellhole, I have your tracker on my phone. I will slip away from the authorities and rescue you. Know that."

"Michelle, I know that you will; you don't have to tell me that. I know I can absolutely count on you as a partner."

"Thank you. It was a different story when we were both inside the United States, but we don't have any standing here. I'll also try to dismantle any shore-patrol boats before we depart on the sailboat. That might give us the running start we need. Of course, if all this happens, we won't at all have completed our mission for the CIA. I might have to come back on my own to see what I could do here."

"I know you feel untouchable because you can teleport to anywhere at any time, but you could still get hurt here and we're partners; you are not completing this mission without me."

"You are so sweet, Jason. Do you think they disabled our sailboat? Should I go take a look right now?"

"That's a good idea. Let's look at the cameras to make sure the dock is clear. Our boat sitter should be onboard, so you don't want to be seen on the boat."

"Okay, what am I looking for in the boat?"

"The coast is clear right now on the dock; there is no one standing around. Check the fuel level, the cables at the back, and the battery. If those three things are good, we can make it out."

"Got it."

Michelle was gone for about seven minutes. They had left the new illegal camera untouched, so Michelle stepped into the bathroom before teleporting to their sailboat. When she returned, she again walked out of the bathroom and sat down.

"The gas and battery levels are good. Our sitter is nowhere to be found. As far as I can tell, they pulled the cable that connects the fuel tank to the engine. So, I'll just grab one off of another boat when we're ready to go. Of more concern is they put a heavy chain with a lock on it connecting the boat to the dock. I'll need to fetch some bolt cutters when we're ready to leave. I'll ask Sheila to put them in my apartment in Virginia so I can pop in when the moment is right. I might also have her put some additional cables just to make sure we have got everything when we shove off. What should we do now? Do we go out to a restaurant and nightclub tonight like nothing is going on? How do we get more information out of the woman at the port if we leave too soon? Should I gather up some disguises for us?"

"Those are some good ideas and suggestions, Michelle. Let's talk through the disguise question because we need to act on that fast if we're going to do it. You could take anything of value in this hotel room over to our suite in Curaçao so we can walk away from the hotel room. As they've seen our Panamanian passports, we have to assume they have pictures of us. I think you have a good idea about the disguises. We can darken my skin tone and hair and lighten yours or grab a wig. I'll need some different clothes to put on twenty pounds or so, as will you. Let's give Sheila a ring and ask her to gather all of that up for us in the next thirty minutes because I feel like the clock is ticking and we might meet up with storm troopers at any moment."

They carried out the plan that they talked through. They left stuff behind in the hotel room as they exited through a stairway and then out a balcony on the lower floor. They headed for the nearest Metro station and took a train to another stop, before hailing a taxi back to the city where their boat was located. There wasn't anywhere close to the boat to hide, but there was a hill that provided surveillance of their boat through binoculars. They rested under the tree watching for any activity. They assumed at some point someone would notice their departure from the hotel and immediately look for them to show up on the boat.

They were grateful for the shade of the tree because the disguises they were wearing increased their body heat, which wasn't a good thing in a tropical climate made worse by an impending rainstorm. Fortunately, they had plenty of water to drink to make up for the loss of it through sweat. They spied a guard at the entrance to the dock where their boat was tied up. He seemed to fall asleep in the heat of the late afternoon.

"I assume they'll have someone else to guard the dock at night," said Michelle. "I haven't seen anybody on our boat, so I'm guessing our sitter was ordered to leave by the authorities. Once it gets dark, I'll pop down there with the bolt cutters and cut the chain. I'll make sure everything is still ready to go and reconnect that one cable. How about if I fetch you an inflatable kayak or raft and you make your way to that point near the exit to the marina and hop aboard the boat there? That will get you by the guard."

"That will work. We could also just knock out the guard."

"I'd rather not increase the charges against us if we're caught. I'm glad that we sailed away from several other locations, so I know what to do. I'd hate to try and steer that boat away from the dock for the first time. As it is, I won't relax until I meet up with you."

"Right now, we need a raging rainstorm and darkness. I think as soon as it's dark, you should start throwing cables into the water from every boat you can find in this port area before we approach our own boat. Looking around this area, there might be upwards of fifty boats that you need to disable. Do you want to take a nap now as we'll have a lot of adrenaline-filled moments once darkness arrives?"

"I would love to take a nap, but I'm too hot and too nervous. I will leave the surveillance to you and close my eyes to give them some rest, but I can't imagine that I'll get any sleep. I'd go find an air-conditioned room to nap in, but that would leave you by yourself and if you had to move or were captured, it would be harder to find you. So, in the end, I wouldn't get any sleep anyway."

"I'll keep watch."

"By the way, what's the real story of what you saw during our tour? I forgot to ask."

"I saw a person carrying a bottle of fruit juice that looked similar to the one you found in that refrigerator near the port. So, I followed the person for a while to see what they were up to. They entered an apartment building and I couldn't follow, so I returned to you and the tour guide."

"You didn't by chance take a picture of the building? I could go inside right now and check it out," Michelle said.

"Let's not distract ourselves with that right now. I just want to get away from this country tonight. Then we'll regroup with Langley and figure out what to do next in pursuit of this new illicit drug disaster waiting to arrive on American shores. I did get a picture of the building, so we can pursue that at a later time."

"What's your guess on the type of apartment building it was? Were you in an impoverished area? Was it perhaps middle-class or was it a luxury building?"

"Here's a picture. It's a tall residential building that looks like it's owned by a slumlord. There are so many apartments, there's no way anyone could figure out where the guy with the bottle of fruit juice went. So, it's a dead end as far as I'm concerned. We'll have to watch out for those bottles of fruit juice until we understand what they are. Maybe there's something innocent, but I never like a coincidence. I find it odd that we would see two bottles so similar in shape and color without any labels on them carried by different people in different parts of the country. The port and Caracas are only nine miles apart, but it's a different world in the big city compared to the port. Maybe some spy satellite can figure out what the bottles are for."

"Even someone with my teleportation skill would be unable to figure out which apartment the person lived in. It looks like the building is twenty stories and at least twenty apartments across the side of the building. I agree with you in your decision to abandon following the guy."

"Someone's down at the dock. It looks like they're changing shifts between the guards," Jason said looking at his watch. "The shift must start at four and perhaps go till midnight. The feeling I get reading about Venezuelans in the military or the government is that they're doing it to support their families and they know they'll lose everything if they show one moment of disloyalty toward the government."

"So we make our move at midnight. What would you like me to fetch for you to get you out to the boat?"

"I'm tempted to just swim out to the boat."

"What if the water is rough? Or there is an undertow, or more likely there's pollution because that's probably the way Venezuela operates. I could bring you a scuba suit with fins, mask, and snorkel."

"Let me check the area out a little more with these binoculars. I like your idea of the scuba suit. It's dark and it will be hard to see me in the water. If I'm standing up on a paddleboard, I make a nice target. It would be better if you could fetch me a sea scooter; even though it's small, I would reach the boat faster. It's too bad the authorities took ours with them."

"I'll drop Sheila a list of items."

"The sea scooter operates on battery, so make sure she charges it before you get there. It should fit in your large duffle bag."

Michelle sent her list to Sheila and said she would be there to pick things up in about three hours. She asked Sheila to make sure the sea scooter was charged. Hopefully, their local large sporting goods store had such an item, or maybe they would have to find a scuba shop.

There was no more activity at the boat and Michelle began making multiple trips to Virginia and back. On one of the trips, she brought back hot macaroni and cheese and cold ginger ale sodas. The carbohydrates were good, and they might not be eating for a while. If Michelle had to throw it up later when she was seasick, at least it was soft coming out of the back of her throat. Jason gave her a pained look when she made that remark to him.

After they had everything they needed and it was dark, Michelle and Jason made their way to the point at the edge of the marina where she would pick him up. He was already wearing the wetsuit as it was black and helped hide him in the darkness. Michelle was wearing waterproof pants and a jacket. The winds had picked up and were rocking the boats and it was raining hard. The guard at the dock's entrance had moved back to the marina office. He was still outdoors, but no longer in direct rain. Michelle and Jason verified that their comms worked, and she left him lying on his belly trying to keep a low profile and waiting for when she got the boat going. He would enter the water at the same time she left the dock; they just needed to find each other on the water in the dark in the howling rain. The sea scooter could go the same speed as the sailboat as it was leaving the marina.

Michelle spent the next hour teleporting from boat to boat disabling engines and throwing the cables into the water. She reached the area where the shore-patrol tied up its boats. There was lighting shining on the boats that might pick up her dark shadow, but she was so quick to pull the cables off that by the time anyone watching focused on her for a second look, she would be gone. She disabled everything she could find but she knew she couldn't touch the naval ships. They didn't have the simple motors for her to reach and there were men on board. But their base was a little farther away and if they sailed toward Colombia rather than straight north, they might be harder to find. Of course, since Venezuela was doing drug running for Colombia, the two countries were friends and they might end up with two navies searching for them, but they would worry about that if it happened. Michelle was counting on disorganization, a rainstorm, and darkness to allow them to escape.

She let Jason know that she was returning to their sailboat and for him to get into the water. She teleported near the marina office to check on their guard and was happy to see he'd fallen asleep in a chair. From there she traveled to the deck of their sailboat. She briefly checked the two rooms and found their sitter absent. That was good news. The last thing they wanted was someone calling for the guard. She dropped a little acid on the chain and then used the bolt cutters. She let the chain silently sink to the bottom. She turned the engine on and was happy to hear it kick over. She quickly untied all the ropes holding it to the dock and began backing up. She glanced toward the guard, and he still looked like he was in a sleeping position. His career would end with tonight's boat departure. She moved out of the slip and quietly motored toward the point. Jason and the sea scooter had lights on to help her see him in the water. She was so relieved to see the lights ahead. She threw the ladder over the side and slowed the boat and helped him aboard. This was no easy feat as the boat was rocking from both the storm and meeting the greater Caribbean Sea.

# CHAPTER 13

*M*ichelle gave Jason a quick hug, relieved beyond her imagination to hand the boat over to him in the storm.

"Thank you. Let me do a quick check of everything then I'll take over. Maybe you can bring up some gear for me so I can get out of this wetsuit. Then I'll want you in front of the boat's mast for the next couple of hours. Please put a life preserver on. If you feel yourself going overboard, teleport back by my side."

Jason was shouting to be heard over the wind.

Michelle nodded and saluted, "Ay, ay, Captain."

Jason made a quick run around the boat checking it out. He unzipped the storm sail grateful it was a dark color. In fact, he was grateful the entire boat was made from wood as it was harder to see both by the pirates and whoever else might be coming after them. He was also happy he had taken down the radar reflector which usually sat atop the mast. He'd removed it when they headed into dangerous waters on the way to Venezuela and now, he wasn't faced with getting it down in choppy seas.

The current flowed in a westerly direction at the northern edge of Venezuela. Once they met Colombian waters the current would change to a more northwestern flow, which was perfect to get them back to Curaçao except that it would be a couple of days sailing. It was better to stop in Bonaire. Maybe the agency could find someone to sail the boat back to Curaçao, while he and Michelle found another way back to Venezuela as they hadn't completed their mission. The wind was behind them, and the motor was propelling them along at about eight miles an hour. With the storm-sail up, the boat might make it up to nine to ten miles per hour. They would sail out of the storm in a few hours and daylight would also begin shortly thereafter. They needed to get out of the reach of the Venezuelan authorities. Hopefully, they would assume that they died in the storm, but Jason was a better sailor than that. He checked the radar every fifteen to twenty minutes and they were not on course to hit anything out in the wide-open sea. They or the agency should be able to return this boat to the marina they rented it at in a few days. All he needed to do was steer the boat toward Bonaire. He would add that he needed to stay awake, but the weather was so wild it was keeping him on his toes.

He checked periodically on Michelle and was happy to see her plastered to the mast every time he looked. He wondered if she was throwing up. It was too noisy for him to hear between the wind, the slap of the waves, and the occasional rumble of thunder in the distance. After a few hours, he could tell the storm was easing up. The wind and the rain had slowed, and the waves were softer. He motioned Michelle to come down to the wheelhouse. She dropped on her hands and knees and scooted on her butt until she reached him.

"Only for you would I have stood on a rocking boat being plastered in rain with night vision goggles that were barely any help to see what was in front of me. I was so tempted to teleport to dry land, but I couldn't desert you."

"I am beyond grateful for everything you did. I think otherwise I would have a few bruises and be inside a Venezuelan jail. How is your stomach; did you throw up out there?"

"No. I had such an adrenaline rush wondering if we were going to survive that I forgot to be seasick. It would be cool if that horrible couple of hours glued to the mast forever cured me of getting seasick. I don't want to eat right now, but I didn't toss the mac and cheese. Where are we?"

"Thanks to the wind and a favorable current, we're about twenty-five miles off the coast of Venezuela. In theory, we are in international waters, but they don't follow the rules. The Venezuelan military could run us down, but I don't know if they have a big enough reason to do so. We don't know what made the Venezuelans suspicious of us. Were they worried that we might somehow change the drug market? Did they not believe our story that we were expatriot Americans living in Panama? I'm sure they've seen that story many times. They probably wondered about us being crazy enough to sail into their waters and into their port. So, fingers crossed, they're done with us. We should reach Bonaire in the late afternoon, and we'll definitely be safe in the Kingdom of the Netherlands."

"What can I do to help you?" Michelle asked

"I've been checking the radar every fifteen to twenty minutes to make sure nothing's in our path. We'll need to do that until daybreak and then we can just use our eyes at that point to look for other boats. My navigation system is keeping us away from the offshore Venezuelan islands. We're sailing out of the storm, which is good news for our seafaring survival, but we'll be moving slower without the wind carrying our sail as much."

"Can we put the other sail up to go faster once the wind dies down?"

"I'm hesitant to do that. I'd love to get away from the Venezuelan coast faster, but the other sail is white in color, so we'd best stick with just the storm sail. Once we get a little farther from Venezuela, we'll put the full sails up."

"When did you last check the radar? I'm going to set my cell phone alarm to check it on the schedule."

"Let's do a check now together to make sure you know what you're looking at. In a few hours, I'll also need a break from piloting the boat. We'll be out of the storm by then and I think I'll be so tired that I can sleep on the bench here in the wheelhouse and be close if you need me."

"You should go down below when you're ready to nap. You'll get better sleep down there and I can manage to keep the boat on course and still check the radar occasionally. It will be just like when we sailed south here, only then we were worried about pirates. Hopefully, all the pirates stayed home while the storm was raging, which should give us about a five-hour head start at least. With any luck, some of the boats I dismantled belong to pirates and they'll all have to wait for new cables to arrive before they can go out and attack more boats."

"There is an upside to all that work we did leaving Venezuela: we made the seas safer for everyone for about eight hours. At least it's cooler out here with the light rain and the wind. It was hot sitting on that hillside waiting to leave that country. I've been thinking about how we can return, though, because we didn't complete our mission, and someone needs to. If the agency doesn't send us back, they'll have to send someone else to investigate this new drug. We at least have experience with the country."

"Maybe we need to come in to Venezuela from the east on the next trip. Either from Guyana or Trinidad. The agency needs to figure a way in and a way out. We'll need Venezuelan passports. If the agency knows where Venezuela makes its passports, I could teleport there and make two for us when the office is closed. I'm sure they're not open twenty-four hours a day."

"That's a good idea. We want to do some work on our faces, so the picture doesn't look the same as the Panamanian passport in case they have a record of that. We'll need to send an email to Sheila about our night and our needs. I'd call her on the telephone but it's still early morning at Langley and there's no reason to wake her just because we're doing stuff in the middle of the night."

They checked the radar and saw no boats out there. Then Michelle composed an email with some input from Jason and they sent it off to the satellite that would bounce it down to Langley. She went below to change out of her bulky clothes and raingear to something more suitable for a soon-to-be calm day on the Caribbean Sea. When she knew they would be sailing, one of the things she packed was ginger black tea. It would settle her stomach and give her a little caffeine. She made two cups and brought one up for Jason. He took a sip and made a face.

"I was expecting coffee. Tea is a little jarring."

"Ah, but this is ginger tea with caffeine. So it settles our stomachs and keeps us awake. I can go make you some coffee if that's what you want."

"No, this is okay. We probably both need to replenish our fluids after our activity in the past twelve hours. I forgot to ask since I haven't been below yet, but are our weapons still on the boat?"

"I'll check. They should be as we didn't see the officials leaving the boat with anything other than our technology. I'll go look."

Michelle went below and opened the false bottom where they had stashed weapons. The guns were in there as well as their cache of smoke bombs. Once they reached Bonaire, she would have to go to work moving the stuff back to Langley. It wouldn't do for the Curaçao marina to find their stash.

Michelle yelled from down below as she was closing things up, "The guns are still here along with everything else. I brought a drone aboard in the most recent supply of stuff from Sheila. Once the rain and wind end, do you want to put one up in the sky to see if any boats are streaming out of Venezuela and coming our way?"

She returned to Jason's side as he said, "I doubt the drone can see that far for us. I just wanted to make sure we still had one. If I was less tired, I would have remembered that we didn't see them removing weapons on video. That rain and storm should've cleared the sea of most boats other than the military and cargo ships."

"My phone app says sunrise is in three hours, so we should start to see daylight coming from the east in about two and a half hours before the actual sunrise."

"Yes, I'm looking forward to that. It will mean that we're probably another twenty-five miles away from the coast of Venezuela. If they really want us, they will send military aircraft out to look for us, and let's hope they stay grounded for a while."

"Is there anyone the agency can call to give us an escort into Bonaire?" Michelle asked.

"That's a good question. Why don't you do a search for that on Google? I'm not familiar enough with where we have military installations around the world."

She did as he suggested and was soon smiling.

"Guess what, the United States Air Force has an installation in Curaçao that is supposed to be used for fighting drug smuggling. I think we should get them overhead of us. We're about to find out how much pull the agency has with the military. I'm calling Sheila on this one. I'm nervous as the storm is lessening and it was part of our protection. If we wait until we need their help, they won't get here fast enough."

Jason thought it was an overreaction, but then again, he had underestimated the Venezuelans before. He had to agree with his partner that if they waited to call for help, it would be too late. They were sitting ducks out here in the sea. Then he had a thought.

"We should do a search to see if they left any trackers on board. What did you do with the scanner from the hotel?"

"I dropped it into our suite in Curaçao. Just a moment, I'll retrieve it."

Jason had a huge grin on his face when she appeared perhaps a minute later.

"What? What are you smiling about?"

"I'm smiling at what a great partner you make. There's nothing you can't do."

"Yeah right. I can't act to save my soul. You have that strength and it's been critical to your success as a CIA case officer."

"Yes, but your way is so much sexier. Here, take the wheel; I'm going to do a scan of the boat. Then we'll call Sheila. If we find any, we can only hope that the trackers are out of range or they got wet in the rainstorm."

"Grab the drone while you're at it. If you find one, we should use the drone to drop it far away."

"What an excellent idea!"

Jason came back with a tracker in his hand and set the scanner down.

"I just had another thought. The marina we rented this boat from would have been wise to install a sensor. It's still the middle of the night so I can't call and confirm, but I'll do so once we reach office hours. I'm going to take a picture and video of it and then use the drone to drop it at as far a range as it will handle."

As soon as he deposited the device in the sea, they placed the call to Sheila and explained the past twenty-four hours.

"Let me handle your first issue first and then I'll call you back," their boss said before hanging up.

They were completely out of the storm and were unfurling the sails when they heard their satellite phone ring.

"I had to pull some strings on this request. Fortunately, you're in an area of drug trafficking so it's much easier to excuse why an Air Force jet might be hovering over a tiny sailboat. I understand you should hear them in about five minutes. They asked for an update of your location."

Jason relayed their coordinates and both he and Michelle looked to the northern sky knowing that sound travels faster than planes. They could see the lights in the distance and hoped that was their protection arriving. Michelle turned to look at the radar and caught more lights out of the side of her eye. She looked to the south and also saw lights.

"Can you tell the plane that there are also lights coming in from the south and we would appreciate their arrival sooner rather than later!"

They could tell they were on hold from the buzz of the connection as both sets of lights continued to approach the boat. They were pleased to see the lights from the north seeming to speed up, so they were almost overhead as the lights from the south approached. It was the only noise beyond the wind and waves in the middle of the Caribbean Sea. It was so loud that they couldn't hear anything Sheila said. They kept the camera focused on the sky above them and connected a second satellite phone so they could text.

*CIA: The Air Force plane has made contact with the other plane. It has identified itself as the Bolivarian Military Aviation. They say they have orders to escort your boat back to Venezuela as you are escaped criminals.*

*Michelle: How can we be criminals if we were never arrested or charged?*

*CIA: Our Air Force has made clear that you are in international waters and under their protection.*

*Michelle: Sheila, thank you for getting the jet there. We'd likely be dead otherwise. Can you find out what we have been charged with?*

*CIA: The people on board the plane say they don't know what your charges are, but that you were armed and dangerous.*

*Michelle: In a sailboat by ourselves in the middle of the ocean? We're just Panamanian citizens trying to return our boat to the marina in Curaçao. We give thanks to our friends the American Air Force for protection.*

*CIA: Aren't you full of bullshit this morning?*

*Michelle: Just trying to find diplomatic words to ease the tension of the situation. The plane to the south seems to be heading back toward the Venezuelan coast. Jason says we won't reach Bonaire until afternoon.*

*How long can the plane stay in the sky? Our speed is about 8 miles an hour and the plane is probably going 600 miles an hour.*

*CIA: You're going to get an escort nearly all the way to Bonaire. The Air Force will do a calculation on when you'll be safe from a Venezuelan plane being dispatched from their coast. Our guys have more than one plane and can switch out as the fuel demands. While in the air, they'll be looking for drug runners and thus pursuing their mission.*

*Michelle: I think we can hear you now over the other satellite phone and we have more to discuss.*

They turned off the phone that they were using to text with and resumed talking with Sheila.

"Sheila, we didn't come close to completing our mission of finding the drug source in Venezuela. We think we need to re-enter the country from the east with some disguises and Venezuelan passports. If you can find the office that makes those passports, I'll teleport there and make ours. Can your analysts develop another way for us to return to Caracas? Jason saw a second bottle being carried by a citizen that looked like the one I dropped off at Langley. That person was walking into an impoverished building, which has us wondering if the government is testing it on unknowing subjects."

"We found someone in the CIA who can charter your boat back to Curaçao. They will be arriving in Bonaire tomorrow morning. The tracking device that you found on your boat is a very common device worldwide, so we don't know if it came from the Venezuelans or the boat owner. I would advise that once the marina opens this morning you call them and ask about the tracking device and let them know that someone else will be bringing back the boat. Is it undamaged?"

Jason grinned and replied, "It is now that the U.S. Air Force is flying overhead. Thirty minutes ago, it could've been blown out of the Caribbean Sea."

"It's good to know the agency won't be paying for a new boat."

"Or our funerals," Michelle muttered.

"I'm very pleased that the two of you are alive and willing to continue this mission. Let there be no mistake about that. Michelle, you've offered some suggestions that need to be researched here so we can figure out a new game plan. As soon as you secure the boat in Bonaire, head to the airport to catch a flight to Curaçao. You'll be comfortable in the suite while we develop a plan here. I'm sure you're exhausted after the last twenty-four hours and would appreciate a little bit of a break before we send you back to Venezuela. That will give HQ twenty-four hours to come up with a plan including perhaps your idea of making passports. Michelle, you wanted a vacation in a tropical place after your assignment rescuing our captain in frozen Siberia. Here's your chance."

"No offense, Boss, but one day does not make a vacation. Still, I'll take what I can get."

"You'll hear back from me tomorrow sometime and hopefully we'll have a plan figured out or you'll be subject to a second day in paradise."

# CHAPTER 14

*I*t was a comforting ride over the next eight hours or so when they saw occasional flyovers by the Air Force plane. As they got close to Bonaire, Jason started making a few calls about renting a slip. They found one available at the port of Bonaire, which was conveniently located next to the airport. They were back in their suite in Curaçao by dinnertime.

"I don't know about you, but I'm exhausted. I spent a lot of adrenaline between our escape from Venezuela, to navigating the boat through the storm, through the tension until the Air Force came to our rescue. I'd like to find a place that will deliver food to us. Then I'll take a shower and sleep till tomorrow morning," Jason said.

"That sounds like an excellent suggestion as I'm exhausted too, but I know a nutritious meal would also do me good. Let's arrange that and call it an evening."

The next morning, a CIA operative landed in Bonaire and boarded the boat for the two-day ocean cruise to Curaçao. He and Jason had a brief phone call about where everything was as well the name of the slip he needed to return the boat to. Just as they were ending the conversation, the operative said, "This is my best agency assignment ever."

Jason just shook his head thinking about all that they had been through in the last couple of days. He also knew this was the peace before the storm as getting back into Venezuela wouldn't be easy. Today, though, all they had on their agenda were two snorkeling expeditions, one in the morning and one in the afternoon. There were some great dive spots around the island and Michelle had a wonderful time floating among the fish and not worrying about whether she and her partner would be alive at the end of the day, or perhaps worse, jailed in a Venezuelan prison.

They made their way back to their hotel suite exhausted from what they saw underwater and in the endless sun. After they got rid of the seawater and sweat, they planned to go out to dinner and enjoy a gourmet meal. If they reentered Venezuela from the east, they might have to transverse through rain forests. They wouldn't be eating this well again for a while.

They were just about to leave for their restaurant reservation when Sheila called. While Jason answered the phone, Michelle called the restaurant and moved the reservation back a half hour.

"We've made a plan, but we want to study overhead satellite images for a day or two first. We don't want to send you there and have you hang out and question people about this new drug. We need more specific information that is worthy of your risking your lives for. We're convinced the manufacturing of this new drug is occurring on the outskirts of Caracas. There would be space there to grow jimson weed and to build a manufacturing building that will produce synthetic fentanyl as well as process this weed. Our analysts are studying the satellite feed as we speak and we're moving additional satellites into place to look at this area.

"We like your idea of making Venezuelan passports. There's a US embassy on the island and we've made arrangements for them to show you how they do replacement passports. The person who does that has been sworn to secrecy knowing that you are on a mission for your government. You have an appointment with her at seven o'clock tomorrow morning. We want the training to take place before the majority of people arrive at the embassy. Our analysts are looking for locations in Venezuela that make passports. We also have an artist who has subtly changed your appearances. Michelle I'll need you to teleport to my office at the end of this call to pick up the things you need to alter your appearance. If you'll take a portrait of each other, the passport office will produce pictures that can be placed in your Venezuelan passports. I think that covers all the bases. Questions?"

"Any thoughts as to how we're going to get into the country?" Jason asked.

"The agency is working on that topic as we speak. There's a weekly ferry that runs between Trinidad and Venezuela. We may put you on that. It travels across the Gulf of Paria. From the Venezuelan coast, you have about three hundred-fifty to four hundred miles to reach Caracas. We may fly you or we may obtain a car for you. We're also looking into the trains, but that looks hopeless. The infrastructure in the country has fallen apart. We'll have a budget hotel outside of the city for you to stay at and a dossier that describes your life in that country."

"So, what's our extraction method?"

"We're moving naval ships into the region that have helicopters aboard them. They can fly in and pick you up."

"So, you guys think that Venezuela is just going to roll over and let you pick us up?" Michelle asked.

"No, but that's for bigger people than me to figure out. I think the US is thinking that if Venezuela is about to unleash a new drug on the world, then the International Court of Justice in The Hague will stand behind our destroying it and rescuing our people."

"This is starting to get way beyond my pay grade. Do you have something simple for us to solve for the agency?" Jason asked. He felt better knowing about their sailboat nearby, but now they would have nothing except a rescue by air. He and Michelle would talk it over after the phone call ended to see if they could think of any other way to be rescued.

"I think we need some more people to help us with this mission. What if we find where they are growing the jimson and we get captured before we can communicate with Langley?" Michelle asked. "Don't say that I can just teleport home to Langley and tell you what I saw. Jason will be in custody, and we'll need to save him. I'd feel better if there were additional case officers in the country to help."

"We have two assets on the way there now. We're moving them into position to assist you. They've been in Venezuela for three months. It was from them that we first heard rumors of something catastrophic going on besides the economy."

"That's slightly better news," Jason said.

They ended the call shortly after that.

"I wonder why Sheila took so long to tell us there were additional agents in Venezuela?" Michelle asked.

"My guess from my long career at the agency is that she simply forgot. I think she probably has a lot of balls in the air at the moment and at different times of each mission she suffers a little brain damage when she misjudges the ball and it lands on her head."

"Okay, I'll take your answer at face value. I guess we hang around here another day or so enjoying good food and plumbing."

"You've got work to do tomorrow. Remember, you have to make our fake passports. Speaking of which, you're supposed to be teleporting to Sheila's office to pick up our disguises."

"I think my brain is still befuddled from leaning against the mast on a bobbing boat in a ferocious storm. Be right back."

Jason sat on the sofa knowing that she would be right back and the best thing he could do was make sure he stayed out of her way. They hadn't collided yet during one of her teleporting episodes, but it was bound to happen at some point. He checked his watch and decided he better call and move the reservation back another thirty minutes. She wouldn't be long, and they didn't have far to walk, but he was curious to see what the agency had designed to disguise their faces.

He had been leaning back looking at the ceiling thinking about the crazy life he led as a case officer. All of a sudden, she appeared in their hotel suite. She put down a backpack and began pulling stuff out along with two sketches. She sat next to him on the sofa and they both gazed at the sketches of their new faces.

"I understand that Venezuela is thirty-three percent European heritage, thirty-three percent indigenous people heritage, and thirty-three percent from the slave trade. The analysts appear to want to darken our skin and hair to fit in better with the latter two groups. I don't disagree with them based on the people I saw walking around Caracas and in the port cities. I think we both were simply too fair-skinned. It doesn't help that it's spring where we live, and we hadn't gotten that much sunshine until we were on the boat. There's a lotion here that is supposed to be like a spray tan that we'll have to apply about every four days. You and I apparently had braces as teenagers as we have straight teeth, so they've given us some dental implants that will screw up our speaking. We have contact lenses to change our eye color to brown, wigs, clothing, and a little clay to widen our noses. We've got work to do tonight so that we can take pictures before I head to the embassy tomorrow. Let's walk over to the restaurant and get takeout and cancel our reservation."

Jason nodded as he could see they had work ahead of them mastering these disguises and taking pictures. They left and walked to the restaurant, returning with magnificent-smelling food that they ate while studying the sketches of themselves that they were going to try and match.

"I wonder if I can eat with dental implants. Maybe I better try it so I know the answer." Fifteen minutes later she gave up. "My food is getting cold. I guess I won't be able to eat in front of anybody once we're in disguise."

"I've been on missions before where we did disguises, and it was much easier than this. The contact lenses and the dental implants are the killers. Also, wearing a wig in a tropical climate is such a drag."

After they finished their meal, they went to work in front of the bathroom mirror trying to re-create the drawing and skin shade. Michelle's experience in the past with tanning solutions left her orange. They really needed to be on the olive color spectrum, so she hoped the agency's skin dye was better. An hour later they were pleased with the results and ready to take portraits for the fake passports that Michelle would learn how to make the next morning.

"I suppose I'll be teleporting into some office in some city in Venezuela this time tomorrow. I wonder what the agency will find for me there."

"There are a lot of unknowns about this mission, and the deeper we go the more unknowns we confront. I hope the agents who have been there for a few months are a help to us. I guess I should feel optimistic about our prospects once we have these disguises on. They've been there for three months and haven't been discovered, and we came to someone's notice in a day or two."

After taking the pictures, Michelle said, "I suppose I should sleep in this costume, so I get used to it."

"Yes, your disguise needs to be a part of your everyday soul. We'll probably need to walk a little differently to mirror the walk of someone living in high heat and humidity. I think we have the habit of walking like busy Americans."

"I'll tell you, rescuing hostages from situations is so much quicker and fun than these recent missions from the CIA. You're an awesome partner, but I don't like how many unknowns there are and the dangers in the environment."

"There's an expression for you, Michelle."

"What?"

"Suck it up, Buttercup."

"Good night to you too," Michelle returned with a smile and headed to her bedroom to sleep.

For all she knew this would be the last time for a while she would sleep on a nice mattress with clean sheets. She briefly thought about leaving the CIA as she didn't like this assignment. However, having worked with Jason on two cases now, she couldn't just up and leave him, knowing his life could very well be endangered.

She was up early the next morning to head to the US Embassy. She was met at the gate by a woman named Monique St. Clair. She clearly loved working at the embassy and serving Americans who needed something while on vacation.

She walked Michelle through the process and then had her demonstrate back three times. The most complicated part was uploading the information to make the RFID biometric section of the passport. Each time Michelle got significantly faster at creating the passport. Now all she had to do was find the right building in Venezuela to begin printing her own passports. She left to join Jason for brunch at an outdoor restaurant at the beach. The weather, coffee, food, view, and her companion were all exceptional. They were in a holding pattern waiting to be ordered to take the next steps by their boss. They already knew about flights between Curaçao and Trinidad.

"I'm going to look at that ferry schedule. Sheila mentioned it went only once a week. If they choose that as our entry method into Venezuela, there's only one day that we know will be heading out."

Jason watched her for a few seconds and then asked, "What day is it?"

"It's five days from now. So, we either have a few more days of vacation here on this wonderful island, or the agency can find another way for us to get over to Venezuela."

"That's an interesting timetable. I'll admit that I wouldn't mind a few more days break on this island before we head over to Trinidad to catch that ferry. I wonder what kind of surveillance capability Venezuela has of its border? Could the US military drop us off close to the border in Guyana, and then we would have walked through a rain forest and caught a ride?"

"Let's not worry about that just yet. My experience in prior cases is that the agency does a good job planning so I'll save the what-if's until they give us a plan. About the only thing I know is that we won't be walking as it would take us too long. Before we get instructions, someone at the agency will know more about Venezuela than we do."

"That's true. In that case, maybe we should go play in the water again. I'll have to remember how clean I felt while in the water when many days go by in Venezuela and I don't have the opportunity to have a shower. Yuck," Michelle said.

They did as Michelle suggested and frolicked in the water that afternoon. They had another call with Sheila in the early evening, during which they received instructions on where Michelle was supposed to go to make their two passports. The CIA looked at the various cities of Venezuela that made passports and there were few. They put a hacker to work to hack into the IT system where Venezuela registered its passports. Michelle had a login and password so she could complete the work of registering the new passports. The CIA knew when the office was open and closed and what security they had in the specific room where passports were made. They even went so far as to give her a signature to copy of the person who made passports in that office.

Around midnight, she would be teleporting into that office to make the passports for the two of them. The biggest danger would be the minimal light Michelle would need to make the passports, and the light from the monitor when she logged into the IT system. Their gadget department made Michelle a long skinny flashlight that would shine on only the document that she was working on. Likewise, they had a screen for the monitor that would greatly dim the lights that shone from it but would still allow her to see words. That hacker had also written down in Spanish where she would have to go inside the IT system to register the passports. After she entered their passports into the system, the hacker would go back in to change the time on the computer so it looked like her login was done during the daytime when the employee would be there. It was a lot of technical instructions for her to master in a short time. She had Jason quiz her on reading the application questions in Spanish, so she would be as fast as possible when the time came later that night.

They had another great meal in Curaçao, and then Michelle and Jason spent time working on their Spanish language fluency. Finally, the midnight hour arrived, and Michelle was ready to go with their pictures in her pocket and copies of their fingerprints, as well as instructions. This might be the oddest thing she had done so far in her career as a CIA case officer. She teleported out of their suite, and Jason found himself pacing in her absence. She expected to spend no more than half an hour in the office, but if she ran into problems, she would teleport back to the hotel suite to update him and go back. That was the plan.

# CHAPTER 15

$\mathcal{M}$ ichelle teleported into a government office. She was glad her teleportation talent could find her a location in the dark. She arrived with two flashlights—one to walk around the office with, the other to look at documents. The office flashlight was a very low beam, just enough so she didn't trip. She quickly found what she needed to create the passports and went to work. She finished the passport part and then went to work on the computer system. It was a shame the hacker couldn't do all the work for her, but there was an RFID scanner to scan the passport, so she understood why it had to be completed inside the office. She just added their names and then heard a noise.

The analysts didn't mention that there was a security patrol. She hit the button to turn off the monitor, shut down her headlamp, and looked for a place to hide. Milliseconds later she was tucked underneath a desk in the far corner. The door opened and someone walked in. She nearly had finished everything making their passports. She had two more things to complete the process. Darn, she hoped the man would leave soon. She had the two passports in her pockets, but she needed another two or three minutes in the IT system. She watched as shoes approached where she was hiding, and she thought it was likely a female. Once the shoes began walking away from her, she snuck a glance to see who was there.

She was puzzled by what she saw and watched for a few minutes, then she smiled as she realized what she was looking at it. Someone else broke into the office and was also making fake passports. She debated what to do: Help the woman or wait until she finished and come back? She watched the woman to see how many passports she was making. There were ten. She seemed really comfortable in the room. So much so that Michelle wondered if it was the woman's day job to work in this office. Maybe she took bribes to process passports. She looked at her watch and realized she needed to appear back at the hotel suite or notify Jason that she was running late, but otherwise safe. She decided to text and fortunately, she had turned her phone's screen brightness way down before she got here.

*Running late. Female stranger in the room also making passports. I'm hidden and watching her.*

*OMG. We didn't plan for that.*

*Either she works in this office, or she's made passports before.*

*Will she find your hiding spot?*

*No. Besides, I see no weapons. I turned off the monitor before she came in and removed the screen, but if she works here, she'll notice soon that the computer is already on, and the program is open. Can you contact the hacker and have him take the system down? If she is at all knowledgeable about the IT system, she'll see our recent passport entries.*

*Will do.*

She periodically peeked at the woman, knowing that at any moment she would go over to the computer and notice that it was already on. Finally, she did, and then she hit a few more keys and then a few more keys. Michelle was tempted to teleport behind the woman so she could see what was on the computer, but she was afraid when she teleported back to the desk that she would bang her head and alert the woman to her existence. Michelle smiled for the second time that night when she saw the woman unplug the computer, count to ten, and power up.

Michelle cheered silently knowing their hacker got through and screwed up the IT system. She hoped he could straighten it out so she could finish her entries once the woman departed. She needed less than five more minutes with the machine. She relayed what was happening to Jason via texting.

*Can IT make the computer work again once I give the signal?*

*Let me ask. . . . The hacker will send you instructions in an email. It will take extra time but cover your trail well.*

*Okay, thanks.*

After half an hour, the woman gave up and left. Michelle texted Jason with the update. After another twenty minutes passed, she crawled out from under the desk and stretched. She was too old to be scrunched under a desk for an hour. She pulled up the email from the hacker and had the computer fixed in no time. She finished her work, shut everything down, and teleported back to the hotel suite.

Jason was startled when she arrived.

"That took way too long, but I guess we should have expected something like that. The corruption in the Venezuelan government is incredible and people desperately want passports to leave the country and establish themselves elsewhere. It makes you wonder if the person making the passports was the one who worked in the office or just some other enterprising person who figured out how to make passports and sell them for big dollars."

"Yeah, I was sweating bullets hoping the hacker would crash the computer. If it was the person who regularly worked in that office, she would figure out in no time what was going on and be able to stop or flag our passports. If she was a criminal making those passports, she would not have cared about other recent passports, but we couldn't take that chance. I want to check with our hacker just to make sure we left no tracks."

Jason gave her the phone number he used to get their emergency intervention into the IT system. Michelle thanked him for his effort and was happy to hear that it all looked good.

"Boy, am I bushed. I blew through adrenaline when I heard someone approaching the office. When I saw what she was up to and that she had ten passports, I knew I would be there a while. I thought about teleporting back here, but I was afraid that when I returned to that office I would bang my head on the desk that I was hiding under. Someday I'll construct a foam fort at home and try teleporting into it to see what my location accuracy looks like. I knew if I made a noise from my head banging against wood or letting out an 'ouch,' the game would be up."

"I was burning through adrenaline worried about you. The fact that you can teleport out of any dire situation doesn't seem to make me relax when I can't see the dire situation that you find yourself in. It's kind of weird that you have the best protection system in the world and yet I don't trust it to keep you safe. Someday I'll get used to it. Let's go get some shut-eye. I think we get to play in the water again tomorrow."

"Playing in the water suits me perfectly. I probably won't be able to sleep in and it's already nearly two in the morning. Good night."

They received word the next day that the agency had booked them on the weekly ferry and they would have another two days of frolicking in the water before catching a flight to Trinidad. The skin dye that they were using was also helped by those days in the sun and they gained a significant olive complexion.

Two nights later they had another video call with Sheila Meeks. She called to give them their orders.

"You know about the flight to Trinidad and the ferry to Venezuela. We have an agent meeting you in a propeller plane. It will make a few stops to gas up on the way to a small airport outside of Caracas. From there you'll take a bus to the cheap hotel we've lined up for you. We have clothing for you to pick up, Michelle, to help you fit in. Our agents will meet you the first day and be at your disposal. I understand they speak better Spanish than you two. Any questions so far?"

They both shook their heads.

"Our satellite analysts have been searching for the greenhouse and manufacturing hub for this drug. Both of them must be fairly large as the plan seems to be that this company is a single source for the world. The analysts have a list of about ten locations so far. We're watching deliveries, people, and the heat of buildings. The jimson greenhouse will likely require twenty-four-hour lights. The manufacture of fentanyl requires the delivery of certain chemicals. We're adding about five locations a day as we continue to analyze photos. By the time you reach your budget motel, you may have thirty sites to check out."

"I'm great at that, but how do I hide my teleportation activity from these two agents? I'm sure they are not stupid," Michelle said.

"The agents are not stupid. You're going to have a bigger list than the one they see. They may each safely check out one building in a day, whereas you could likely check the other twenty-five or so that they know nothing about," Sheila said.

"So, you're splitting Michelle and me up to explore different buildings? That should work. She's much faster than the rest of us and can get out of trouble quicker. That's how we'll keep Michelle's special skill a secret," Jason said.

"Exactly. We think among the four of you, we can locate both the greenhouse and the manufacturing facility."

"And if we find this facility on the first building that we go into, what will be our next steps?" Jason asked.

"Ideally, we would drop a nuclear bomb on the building, but we can't do that. We may send in a SEAL team to rig explosives, or we may have a plan for your team to do something to the building. We're working out what to do with the plants to make sure that they don't reseed and allow Venezuela to concoct this drug again."

"This doesn't sound like much of a plan, but I have to admit it's better than the last one when we were instructed to hang out in the port and hear gossip. When I did hostage rescue, those missions were planned down to the last detail. Now that I have a partner, the situations are much more fluid, and we have to be flexible to prevent world destruction. That probably sounds dramatic, but the thought of millions of Americans and the rest of the globe dying from these miserable drugs is a pretty destructive vision."

"On that philosophical note, I'll let you guys go back to hanging out on a perfect beach."

The call ended and Jason and Michelle looked at each other and then shrugged. It was a dangerous assignment in a dangerous country. Not only would they be enemies of the state if they were caught, but the general chaos of the country also made death a much higher probability than in the worst city in America.

# CHAPTER 16

*C*couple of days later, the plan was proceeding along the steps that Sheila had outlined. They had to wait a few hours to catch a rickety bus to the outskirts of Caracas. They had been able to text with the two additional agents and they would be meeting them in the same hotel. Jason and Michelle just needed to take the final walking steps to reach the budget hotel. They connected with the agents and scanned the room for electronic surveillance. They were finally sitting down to discuss their mission.

"Calling this a budget motel is providing it a flowery description," Michelle said.

They were warned that there frequently was no electricity, and the water came out of the tap in a suspicious color and with not much pressure. They appeared to be sleeping on clean if not heavily mended sheets. There was no air-conditioning and little space. The building was poorly constructed, so sound traveled from the rooms next door and above and from the street. Michelle and Jason had brought batteries with them to keep their technology running. The other two agents were male and were frequently dispatched south of the border given their fluency in

Spanish. This was their first assignment in Venezuela. They had arrived by crossing the border in Colombia, which due to the drug cartels was just as dangerous a country as Venezuela.

They discussed timing, communications, and some things that they were looking for when checking out the building locations. They would have a check-in every hour whenever they were outside of the hotel. The two agents had found some great places to eat, so at least they all wouldn't go hungry. Michelle's clothes were thin and mismatched, but they were clean and that was all she needed. After a long day of travel, they arrived in the late afternoon and planned to survey their buildings after dark that night. They all had dark clothing and even black mouthguards so that nothing showed in the minimal light. They might be walking six to seven miles each night to reach the buildings, and their work would be done at dawn. Michelle knew she would be returning to the hotel with much less exhaustion than Jason and the agents would.

They set off walking and as soon as they began splitting off in different directions to reach their targets, Michelle teleported to her first building. The CIA analyst had sent her a series of images with the front and interiors of the buildings she would be investigating. They didn't have interiors for all of the buildings, so in some cases she teleported close to the building to assess if there was any activity inside in the dead of the night.

Each time they had the hourly check-in, she held her breath that the others were fine. She was averaging about four buildings between each check-in. At this rate, all the locations on the initial CIA list would be investigated that night. She dropped a text to Sheila informing her of this and asking if there would be additional locations. They needed to find the source of these plants, and being close to Caracas made sense. On the other hand, there are many eyes and ears in the largest city of Venezuela, so would it make sense to create this illicit drug operation in a smaller city? She shared that thought with Sheila, who replied that they were looking at additional locations outside of the capital city. If they wanted to move large amounts of the drug, they needed to set up the factory close to a transportation hub in Venezuela or use the existing transportation route set up by the Colombian cartels to move their products through Venezuela and the Caribbean and on to the United States.

As dawn approached, Michelle could be seen walking toward their budget hotel. She knew that the other agents were already there. They had finished searching their one building and didn't have time to do a second one before daylight, so they returned sooner.

After she entered the hotel room, she said "It looks like I'm the slowest to return. I didn't find anything related to the drug trade, did you?" She knew that they hadn't, but it was a way to open the conversation between them.

The other three had seen nothing but idle factories. It was hard to believe that this was such a bustling country fifteen to twenty years ago. Michelle had seen that in many of the buildings she toured, but there were a few that were obviously still producing a product but in a much smaller area.

"We've had word from Sheila that the analysts are looking for additional locations both in and outside of Caracas. Our instructions are to get a good night's sleep for now and I for one am ready to hit the sack. It was a long night and a long walk," Jason said. The other two agents nodded and departed for their own room. Once they were gone Jason had the opportunity to ask Michelle a few more questions.

"How many buildings did you survey tonight?"

"Twenty-eight, and they were all dead ends. The only good thing about my night was I didn't have to walk all the miles that you three did. I hope the agency comes up with a new list by this evening. I'd hate to be killing time in this hotel. People in this country don't have the money to afford multiple nights in a hotel, even one as bad as this one. I'm worried if we stay here too long that the owner will notify someone. I don't know how it works in a really corrupt country. Is everyone in on the scam and reporting people whose behavior is out of the norm?"

"I agree with you. The owner of this hotel owes us no loyalty and has none. He'll probably receive some money from the government for reporting any suspicious activity including whether we are dissidents trying to protest the government. I've been in a few countries that operate on that principle, but I'm not convinced that there is enough love from the Venezuelan people toward their government, nor organization and structure for the government to survey all its businesses. I think it's a toss-up as to whether we're safe here. We'll see if the CIA comes up with more places to explore in or about Caracas or if we move on to somewhere new like Ciudad Guayana. My brief look at that city showed me that they have the potential to operate this drug operation. They have hydroelectric power for the manufacturing and growing process, and the rivers give them access to large boats able to ship this drug to foreign shores."

"Well, for now I'm going to get some sleep, or at least I hope I am. It's hot and it's noisy here, but hopefully I'm tired enough to catch some shut-eye," Michelle said lying on one of the twin beds in their tiny room. The disguise in the heat made the room even more unbearable as she felt like she was sweating just relaxing on a bed.

Michelle managed to doze on and off throughout the day and she drank some cold coffee before their late afternoon huddle with the agents and Sheila.

"We've looked at more satellite images and here's our plan. Michelle will stay for another night in that lovely budget hotel so she can explore one more site in Caracas. She'll then catch the bus and join the three of you in another part of the country—Ciudad Guayana, where Michelle and Jason gassed up their small plane two days ago. We have some buildings to examine there. Gentlemen, if you'll head out toward the bus stop, there is a bus that should be coming by in an hour or so. It will take you near a small airport where a small plane awaits your travel to a remote area near Ciudad Guayana. Once there, you'll have to walk into the city to another budget hotel. This one is much better than the last as it has a pool and air-conditioning."

"That does sound like a step up. That place you booked us last night was an insult to the word "'budget motel"'. The electricity was dubious, as was the trickle of water coming out of the faucet. I guess we better start walking," Jason said.

The threesome wished Michelle good luck and they took off walking toward the bus stop. Jason was sure they were a little puzzled about Michelle being left alone—a female in a violent part of a violent country. Jason told them that she was well-trained in Krav Maga and would be in no danger. He knew she would be checking another twenty or so locations near Caracas and still she would beat them to their destination. She might even knock a few buildings in their new location off the list before they reach the city. The fact that Sheila was having the three of them move on said to him that she didn't have high hopes for any of the locations; otherwise she would not leave Michelle without additional resources. The three of them chatted on the walk to the bus comparing experiences in Venezuela so far. The small plane was too noisy for them to chat, and they mostly nodded off given their late night and poor sleeping conditions.

They landed without incident and were soon checking into a luxurious hotel compared to the last place the agency had put them up. All three of them had fake passports. The two agents had Colombian passports, whereas Jason's was the one that Michelle had made and was as good as a real Venezuelan passport could be. They had paid extra to check in early as they arrived in the early morning after all of their travels. They had a scheduled call with Sheila mid-afternoon and then they would begin work on their next assignment. Michelle was likely already in the area but would text him before she appeared. If she worked all night, she would be ready to crash. So, he sent her a text with a picture of their hotel room and lay down to get some sleep.

When he awoke a few hours later, Michelle was asleep in the bed next to his. She must've dropped in while he was asleep. He looked at his watch and realized he was done sleeping and their phone call with Sheila was within an hour. He decided to let her sleep another half hour and then wake her up for the call. He pulled the curtain aside and looked out the window. There was a family near a pool connected to the hotel, but there wasn't much other activity. After being in the other cities of Venezuela, this city seemed relatively quiet and prosperous. Certainly, there were no signs saying they should expect the electricity to go out, but there was a large hydroelectric dam nearby, so they probably had a convenient form of electricity here. He dropped the curtain and noted it was time to wake up Michelle and so he did.

"Hey, we have a call with Sheila in about twenty-five minutes, the other agents will be joining us here. How did your inspections go last night?"

"Do you have any caffeine? What time is it?"

"I do. I thought you might need some when you eventually showed up. It's coming on three thirty. What time did you get to sleep?"

"I think it was around ten. It wasn't that long after you sent me the text. I checked a bunch of locations in and around Caracas. It was mostly just a sad experience—lots of empty factories. You see all the potential in this country and then you see how its politicians have driven it into the ground and you understand why people try to immigrate anywhere as there's no opportunity here."

"Yeah, I don't understand why there hasn't been a coup to change leadership. This city seems a little more prosperous. Certainly, the utilities are better, unlike our last one-star hotel."

"Have you noticed anyone here acting strange, or have you heard the word *jimson* or seen someone walking around with a bottled fruit juice?" Michelle asked.

"Not yet. We haven't seen much of this town. I'm curious to see what Sheila and the analysts come up with for us to review."

There was a knock on the door. Jason approached it and asked the person in Spanish to identify themselves. He was soon opening the door to let the agents in. They were surprised to find Michelle had arrived.

"I just visited the one place to check out and then like you guys I caught a small plane here. It picked me up closer to our hotel in Caracas, so I didn't waste time walking to the bus stop and taking the bus somewhere. I actually got a good five hours of sleep here thanks to the air-conditioning. Shall we connect with Sheila?"

The four operatives gathered around a satellite phone for the call. Sheila came on the line and had a new list of locations for them to examine for the jimson. She also had an update on the woman that Michelle saw in the passport office. Apparently, she was an employee of that office, but not the one who signed the passports. She returned the next night and entered the passports into the system. The nice thing about that is the person who was in charge of passports wouldn't know the difference between Michelle's two and the other ten.

"Are you seeing this new drug in the US yet? Given its prevalence in Caracas, I would think that would be an indication that supplies were being shipped to the United States," Michelle asked.

"We might be, and we might not notice it. People may be dying, and we aren't testing for jimson. We might be testing for fentanyl, but the woman you spoke with in Caracas said her brother was too sick to take the drug in the few days before he died. I don't know enough about medicine to know if the fentanyl would still show up in a person's blood. If the death occurred and there was a good medical examiner in that county, you would think they would've detected at least the fentanyl. I'll ask my contact at the DEA that question. Maybe they can ask coroners and medical examiners to look out for these kinds of otherwise unexplained deaths."

"Maybe once we find the greenhouse and the manufacturing source, your botanists can determine how old the plants are, and that might at least give us some kind of timeline of how long this drug has been circulating," Jason suggested.

"Yes. I'd like the four of you to start as a team at the top location on the list I'm sending to you. Our satellites have detected around-the-clock heat sources, transportation to and from a building, and it's located on the Caroni River so there's activity at the dock. Our analysts have labeled it the highest probability for this drug's manufacturing which is why we pulled you from Caracas to go to Ciudad Guayana. The Caroni River begins in Ciudad Guayana, and it flows from the Orinoco River which gives any drug sellers access to the Caribbean Sea."

She sent her four CIA agents the street address and they looked at the map on their phones' map to begin planning how to get there. It was a good ten miles away. The city bus system was plagued by a lack of gas and a lack of bus parts. They didn't want to depend on a bus that might never come. One of the agents went down to the front desk of the hotel and asked the person working there how they might get a ride. He came back twenty minutes later to gather up the others for a private ride to a mall that was about three miles away from their intended target. It was perfect. There was a reason for four people to want to go to a shopping mall, and they could spread out and walk without drawing attention to themselves.

"What should we take with us? We need our comms, food, water, and a camera. Weapons?"

"Let's take a taser and pepper spray. I know they have a lot of guns here, but the government banned guns. I'd rather not give them a reason to arrest us for something really lame," Jason said.

"We should also bring flashlights. If you have to use the one on your phone it drains it fast, and it's easier to accidentally turn it on or take a picture with a flash. Let's make sure our phones are on silent and the camera doesn't flash," Michelle said.

Soon they bundled into a small car that had seen better days, but it beat walking on foot. The payment was required upfront. Walking the distance would take time, and they were targets for robbery. The fewer people they had to confront the better. Traffic was light and they were soon at their destination. The driver told them to hurry as the mall was closing soon. He gave them a number to call if they wanted him to return to drive them home. They said it wouldn't be necessary as they were meeting friends for dinner once they ran their errand in the mall. The sun was dropping below the horizon, and they knew by the time they walked the remaining distance to the suspect building, it would likely be dark.

They divided into twos to briefly enter the mall and walk around it. Many stores looked vacant, a sign of the terrible economy in this city and country. They exited and began their walk toward the river and the building they would be surveying.

Sheila had sent them aerial surveillance photos. Before they left the hotel, they decided that the property was a rectangle, and they would approach it from four different angles. As they got closer, dusk was starting, and they added black shirts to cover the clothing they had been wearing for their visit to the mall. They reached the point where they would split off, checking their comms, and doing a silent fist bump before disappearing into the darkening night.

# CHAPTER 17

*A*fter they split up, Michelle decided to do a little reconnaissance on her own to make sure the others would be safe. She teleported inside a few of the buildings, spending no more than five seconds in any location. A couple times she noted that people reacted as though they saw her, but she was so quick to leave it had them doubting their own eyesight. This was the building they were searching for—it had greenhouses and a laboratory. Now she was trying to find the security system. She needed to make the building safe for her teammates. She moved quickly around the building trying to find where a security office might be located, but she wasn't successful. She returned outside and took a moment to send a text to her teammates telling them that she had a positive ID that this was the building generating drugs and to hold their positions while she tried to figure out the security system. She included Sheila in the text, so if they should all die today at least the CIA would know where to find their bodies.

Once she had notification that everyone had received her text, she returned to try and locate a security hub as she knew there had to be one. The crop, the production, and most of all the revenue were too important to leave the building unprotected. She thought she might be running out of time, when she saw the guard in the distance. She teleported behind him and hit him in the head with the flashlight. She felt bad doing that, but she knew the lives of her three teammates would depend on her actions. She took his communications devices off him and put them in her pockets, and then she teleported to where Jason was located.

"Here," she said, handing Jason stuff from her pockets. "I took these comms off a man I conked on the head. I haven't found the security hub yet to see their setup, but I thought it would help if you could monitor the conversation. Can you let the others know while I continue with my search?" He nodded and she was gone.

Jason contacted the other two members of their team via text.

*Michelle has breached the building and been inside. She gave me a security guard's comm. I think we need to gather. Here are my coordinates.*

Jason waited a bit and then he received two texts.

*On my way* and *yes.*

Then he received a third text from Michelle.

*Found the security room. Enrique has been captured by a guard. Going to him for rescue. We should back away from this compound and chat with Sheila. Once Antonio reaches you, retreat.*

Jason wondered what was going on that Michelle could see somehow. All he could think was that she must've found the room where all video feeds were on camera and saw that Enrique had been captured.

A short time later, Antonio texted him that he was almost at his coordinates. Jason got ready to move out when he saw a shadow moving. Fortunately, when the shadow moved closer, he noted it was Antonio.

Jason leaned in and whispered, "We need to back away from this compound. Michelle saw Enrique captured. She's going to intercede and hopefully, the two of them will be free. Let's move at least a half a mile away and then we'll text her with our coordinates."

Antonio likewise leaned in and whispered back, "Maybe we should go back and help. She's just one woman; are you sure she won't get captured?"

"I'm very sure. I've seen her in the heat of battle. Not only will she be safe, but so will your partner."

With that statement, they hustled away and back toward the downtown area of the city. They found a big tree that offered them a lot of cover, and there they waited for Michelle and Enrique.

Michelle had raced around what looked to be an administrative building as she tried to find where the security people were housed. If any cameras were surveying the property, there would have to be a video feed going somewhere. She found the room and, in fact, it was staffed by two men staring at cameras. Fortunately, it was approaching midnight and they had a boring job to do. They were nodding off to sleep before shaking themselves awake. She looked at the screens a little bit and noted her colleague being marched at gunpoint toward the building. As she was looking for the security room, she had passed a circuit breaker. She imagined that circuit breaker in her head and she was soon standing in front of it. She flipped it off, and all around her went dark. She heard people mumbling but knew it was time to teleport to where Enrique was on the move.

She teleported behind the guard and then conked him over the head with the same flashlight she used on the other man. Enrique turned around and was thrilled to see his captor on the ground and Michelle emptying bullets out of the gun the man had been holding. She left him with his gun and grabbed Enrique's arm and said, "We need to go."

He followed her but asked, "Why? Where are Jason and Antonio?"

"This is the building we're searching for. They're growing

jimson weed inside and they have a fentanyl laboratory. However, it's very well protected. We need to retreat and make a decision on what to do next with Sheila's input. The four of us, no matter how skilled, are not going to take over that building as evidenced by you being captured. I've conked two security people in the head and that's going to be noticed. I also managed to pull a breaker box which should make life inconvenient for a while."

"Thanks for the rescue. I wasn't looking forward to being beaten up for information. We just got a text from Jason, and he's provided us the coordinates of where they are located. My map shows us taking a right here and we'll meet up with them in perhaps four minutes."

She nodded and they hustled toward the other two team members. There was a quick flash of light near the tree, and they headed that way.

There were fist bumps for Michelle successfully rescuing Enrique. She recounted what she saw and did while she was inside the building. The two newest members of the team were awed that she had moved so fast through the facility. Like her, they were concerned with the two men who were conked over the head. The operators of the plant would know something was up and likely increase security. Michelle may even have been captured on video in her travels.

"I think we should head back to the hotel. I'm just not sure how to get there at this time of night," Michelle suggested.

Antonio looked around and said, "I think I can help. I'm an expert at hotwiring cars. I'll have us in one in no time. I'll drop you guys off and dump the car somewhere where the owner can find it."

"That will work as long as we don't get caught," Jason said.

"I haven't seen a single police vehicle since we arrived in the city, so I'm not worried," Antonio said. "Besides, with all the damage Michelle did at that factory, I'm sure any cops would be working on finding out who clobbered those two security guards."

He was right. With Enrique's help, they found their way back to the hotel. Antonio dropped them off a block away and then went to a used car parking lot and parked the car. He jogged back to the hotel and the four operatives were soon on a call with Sheila. Michelle for a few seconds had sympathy for her boss as they must be waking her out of her sleep given that was after approaching eleven at night in Virginia. Michelle transmitted pictures from inside the facility to her colleagues and boss.

"Can you have the botanist confirm that the plant they are processing in the video is jimson? If it is, we have our source. There was a growing room and also a lab that might have been making fentanyl. Everyone in it was wearing a respirator over their head. You would have to do that with fentanyl; otherwise, the smell and fumes would knock the employees unconscious, right? They're making something in that building."

"We'll analyze the pictures. Perhaps you could sneak back into the growing area and grab a leaf?" Sheila suggested.

Enrique and Antonio were surprised at Sheila's suggestion, but Michelle just shrugged and said she'd give it a try.

For the two agents' benefit, Sheila added, "We have a plane ready to leave your location with a sample as soon as you get one. Did you see what the final product looked like? Was it a liquid, a powder, a capsule?"

"I didn't see the drug in its final form or if I did, I didn't recognize what I was looking at. I'm afraid to get close given that they're mixing it with fentanyl. In one room, the employees were wearing significant protective wear. I assume that fentanyl was either being made or it was being added to the jimson weed."

"That's a good point, Michelle. Those people are working with dangerous chemicals. We should probably supply all of you with Narcan to reverse the fentanyl in case you come into contact with it. I'll get some delivered to you."

"Include instructions on how to use it. None of us has ever had to use it," Jason said.

"We're in the process of setting up a team to take down that factory. I'm working with the military who are in the Caribbean Sea. I'd love to do more than that. I'd love to follow the transportation routes so we could shut those down too. I'm sure that not only does this designer drug take those routes, but it's also how cocaine travels from Colombia to Venezuela through the Caribbean to the US."

"Can you get a hacker into the systems running that building like the lights, ventilation, temperature, and cameras? If we could distract them by ruining their infrastructure, it will slow them down and make it easier for our team and the new Seal team to move about on that property," Michelle asked.

"That's a great suggestion, Michelle. It would be nice to have better control of the premises by tapping into their electronics," Jason said.

"We'll see what we can do on our end, but I don't have high hopes. It's easier to hack into a national system like passports than that of a private business. I would almost expect them to have additional men assigned to security after tonight's activity. One final question—is this the only factory manufacturing this drug in Venezuela? When you're inside, Michelle, see if you can get a sense of the answer to that question. It would be a good thing. We need to eliminate this plant and therefore, we need to know all locations in which it's being grown."

"You probably also need to know the botanist or farmer or whoever created this plant. They have knowledge in their head and can create it again. It just may take time," Antonio said. "This country is desperate for food, money, and electricity. Don't underestimate the need to put food on the table as a reason for creating the plant."

"That's a very good point, Antonio. We need to find out who that individual is, bring them to the United States and give them a farming plot at one of our federal prisons," Sheila said. "While I'm sympathetic to the need to put food on the table, this plan calls for many thousands of Americans to die as part of the plan, and that's not acceptable."

They ended the call and then discussed the timing of Michelle's going back inside the building. Clearly, the other two agents were puzzled as to why Michelle was so easily selected as the team member to return to such a deadly situation, but the two thought it was close to a suicidal assignment and preferred to avoid that.

"I think now is a good time to go back inside the drug factory and answer Sheila's questions. I would think they would add additional security, but that would take time to line up the men to do so. I'm sure they're on alert now, but not with additional people," Michelle said. "Besides, I did such a good job sneaking up behind the men that perhaps they'll think a ghost is at work here. Does anyone know of any tales that might be of use in this situation? We could leave evidence supporting that piece of folklore."

They all did a quick search on their phones.

"Gee whiz, there are a lot of creepy stories about women, but I don't think that any of them perfectly suit our needs. Do you agree?" Jason asked.

He received nods of agreement and Antonio asked, "Do you want me to go get that car I dropped off at the used car lot, or should I acquire a new one?"

"I'm thinking we need to split up. Antonio and Enrique, why don't you go to different hotels. Meanwhile, Michelle and I will check into a new hotel as husband and wife. I think we may be here for a few more days and we don't want to draw attention to ourselves."

"I have a better idea. Let's take over an abandoned building. It won't be as comfortable as these digs, but it is easier to be hidden. Enrique and I do that often in Colombia. Better still if the agency can show us leaving this region on a plane from the airport."

"I'm awesome at sneaking into buildings but terrible at planning an operation in South America. Antonio, I would appreciate a ride and I like your idea of finding an empty warehouse or something for us to hang out in. Preferably you can find one with a toilet, but if not, I'd rather be safe from the Venezuelan government than have my own personal toilet."

"I'll ask Sheila if she can show us leaving from this city, and Michelle, while you're inside the drug factory, the three of us will find new digs. Let's go."

# CHAPTER 18

*I*n under twenty minutes, the team had packed and left a note for the hotel registration staff that they had a death in the family and had to leave immediately along with some cash to soften the blow of the early checkout. They all took a seat in the hotwired car and returned to the tree that served as their rendezvous spot after their first surveillance of the drug-making complex. Antonio returned the car to the original owner's parking space, and they set off on their missions—Michelle breaking into the drug-making factory while the other three looked for new housing late at night.

Michelle started by teleporting inside the room where the plants were grown. She knew Sheila Meeks's office was empty, so she quickly teleported there and dropped off an entire plant. Again, she spent less than five seconds in the plant nursery before getting out. The lights were on in the nursery so the breaker box that she had tampered with either didn't control this area or had already been fixed. From Sheila's office, she teleported to an office she had found in her previous tour of the jimson weed factory that was empty in the middle of the night.

Now she needed to find the drug in its final form. She was

tempted to go back to the security room and see if she could see it on video. She opened the office door a crack to check the lighting. The hallway was dim. Michelle assumed that was because it wasn't occupied at this time of night. She crept forward while filling out a map in her mind of where she was in the building and where the packaging of the final product might occur. The security room should be on the floor below her and so she headed for the stairwell to go to the lower level. While she could have gotten there by teleporting, she risked landing on someone. It was better to get there on her own two legs. She crept down the stairs listening for sounds but heard none.

She came to the opening for the floor and looked and listened for a while. She saw no movement and the lights were back on full, so someone must've figured out the circuit breaker. The door to the security room was closed. Did she risk teleporting behind it? Should she ditch the idea of trying to see the product on video? She didn't see other traffic in the hallway. She decided to creep forward and try the door. It was locked. She teleported inside it and was immediately disoriented. The lights were out, and no one was home. Maybe they were out helping the two men that she conked on the head earlier. Maybe they were even searching for them in the dark. She pulled out her camera and took five minutes of video feed of the entire room. She checked to make sure she was capturing all ten screens. Her technique was good, and hopefully the analysts in Langley would study the video and identify the final product form. She studied the video monitors herself, trying to identify where packaging occurred. Then she heard sounds from the hallway and a key being put in the door. She teleported back to the empty office on the floor above and played the video looking for the packaging area. After another ten minutes of study, she was still unable to find the room in question. She sent a text to Jason to see where he was, and if the other team members were close by. He was searching an empty building that might serve as their new base. He sent her a picture of it so she could teleport to him. She materialized in front of him and held out her phone.

"I'm trying to discover where they package the final product for shipping. I'm looking for that because I'm looking for the final form of the drug. Can you check out these video screens and tell me if you see a production room? I would think they would be worried about thievery in that area, so they would have it on video."

Jason held her phone and watched the video for a while then he handed it back to her. "Maybe they have a different way of monitoring the production room. I think if I was one of these horrible drug lords, I would just put people in the room with machine guns. If the final form of the product is a powder or pills, then anyone with a good sleight-of-hand could steal all kinds of products if you were dependent on someone watching it on video. I think you're going to have to manually search that complex to find the packaging room."

"Okay, thanks. I'll text you when I'm done," Michelle said and disappeared before his eyes.

He liked the building he was in. It was large; and there was a toilet but no running water. They would have to transport water to the site to flush the toilet and he would be willing to do that for Michelle. He liked that an area of the warehouse had empty shelving with leftover Styrofoam which would make a great pillow. In his mind, it would make a great place to sleep as it appeared softer than the concrete floor. The building was about a mile and a half from their targeted drug factory. The building was quiet, so they would hear anybody coming. He texted Antonio and Enrique with pictures to see if they had found anything better. Turned out he had the best find among the three of them and they soon arrived at his location. With the housing set, and Enrique finding a source of water, there was nothing to do but wait for Michelle to return.

Michelle went back to the dark office as it was a relatively safe place. She pulled up the aerial surveillance pictures that the agency had sent for this operation. She knew where the fentanyl was created, where the plants were grown, and where the administrative offices were located. She would bet that the final packaging area had to be close to where the fentanyl was created. It was such a dangerous substance that whoever was running this factory would have to go to great lengths to protect the employees. She thought about where that room was in the scheme of the bigger complex. Their photos also showed a loading dock. Then she pulled up the video feed on her phone again to see if any of it showed the roof. Maybe she should go up on the roof to understand the layout of the complex. She just wanted to make sure that there wasn't a guard up there ready to shoot at her. She decided to take a chance and head to the roof. She looked at one of the surveillance photos and imagined crouching next to a piece of equipment on the roof and then she was there.

She listened and then looked but saw no one on guard. She was careful to teleport around the roof rather than walking as she didn't want her movement heard below in case anyone was listening. From the roof and through a process of elimination, she figured out where the packaging room had to be. She teleported to the ground and stood a moment looking at some open windows up high that had to represent the packaging area. She decided she would hold her breath in case there was fentanyl in the air. That would give her a good minute to look around and hopefully see the final product. She took a deep breath and imagined the other side of the wall that she was looking at.

With her teleporting skill, there was a moment of disorientation when she arrived in a new place. She thought it was probably pure impulse that made her close her eyes when she moved. Now she opened her eyes and looked around her and a second later she was standing in Sheila's office to the surprise of both of them.

"Oh my gosh, I'm sorry. I teleported into the production room in Venezuela. When I opened my eyes, I was facing an automatic weapon. This was the first spot I thought of to get out of the way. I didn't mean to scare you."

"No worries, I'm just happy you're safe. I'm not often here in the middle of the night, but we have a lot going on in Venezuela at the moment. Did you see the product's final form?"

"No, I was facing the guard, which was a good thing as I knew I had to get out of there. What I do remember is that I watched his lips move as though he was saying something. That means he wasn't wearing protective equipment and the product must be safe. I think that means it's either pill form or liquid, as powder causes problems when people inhale tiny flakes of it that have been aerosolized."

"Okay. Time to go back and look. I guess it's good that it's the middle of the night as the guard is more likely to convince himself that you were a mirage. By the way, thanks for taking the whole plant as it makes it easier for our botanist to analyze it."

"When I got into the plant nursery and looked at the plants, it just seemed to make more sense to steal an entire plant rather than breaking off a leaf. The only problem is that I've left evidence that a plant has been stolen while I don't think anyone would've missed a single leaf."

"True, but we're going to shut down that business."

"How? Are you sure that is the only production site?"

"This is about a war on America and the rest of the world. I don't care if the Venezuelans know that we blew up their production facility, and that is what we are intending to do. We will give a warning in Spanish to anyone who wants to run out of the factory. Anyone who doesn't follow those instructions will die with the building."

"There are enough bad drugs in America killing citizens without Venezuela adding more. I hate that the government has decided that this is how they will fix their lousy economy. Innocent people are working in that factory, and giving them a few minutes to get outside is a gift from the United States."

"Back to your question of is this the only production site? I don't know. There are more major cities besides Caracas. We are looking at Valencia, Maracaibo, and Barquisimeto as possible production sites as all three cities had significant industry before Chavez and Maduro destroyed it. I should have an answer later today. Of course, if the Venezuelans watch us destroy their production facility in Ciudad Guayana, they'll rally around other production sites to protect them," Sheila said.

"Okay. It's good to know your plan. I suppose you want us to complete the mission in our current location and move on to those other cities?"

"Yes. I'll schedule a call with your team around midday."

"Okay, let me find a place to teleport back to near Jason, Antonio, and Enrique."

She texted Jason to find a spot to teleport to. He replied with a picture and geo-coordinates, and she was gone from Sheila's office. She ended up in the dark outside a building. There was a door in front of her that she opened. She heard Jason say, "Michelle, we're over here."

She walked inside and said, "This looks like a decent place to hide out for a few days. Is there a toilet?"

"There is and it's connected to the sewer system but is not connected to water, so you have to refill the tank every time you flush. Still, you got your wish."

"Where's the water?"

"Antonio found a convenient water source outside, so we don't have to haul water a long distance," Jason said. "How did your exploration go?"

"It went well until I walked into a room with a man holding an automatic weapon. I nearly had a heart attack. However, he had his eyes closed and I was able to back out without a sound."

"So, what does the final form of the drug look like?" Antonio asked.

"I don't know. The man with the gun was in the room and I

backed out too quickly to notice. However, he wasn't wearing a mask or any kind of respiratory protection, so that suggests to me that the final form is not a powder. It's either a liquid, an injectable, or in a pill."

Jason looked up from his phone and said, "Sheila has scheduled a meeting with us midday. She suggested we just stay in the building, and she'll talk to us in about eight or ten hours."

"Did you get the plant leaf?" Enrique asked.

"I did. Sheila asked me to leave it in a particular spot for her courier to pick up. I assume it's on its way to Langley. Boy, am I bushed. I used up all of my adrenaline when I saw the man with the gun who could slice and dice me up. Point me to where I should make a bed."

Jason took her over to the area that they all agreed was the best for sleep with the rolls of Styrofoam for pillows and they all tried to get some sleep for what remained of the night. Unfortunately, it was the rainy season in Ciudad Guayana and it was hot and muggy. Rain was expected at any moment. Michelle knew she'd feel better just stretching out and closing her eyes even if she didn't get any sleep. She could feel sweat running down her neck underneath her hair. Still, at some point, she fell asleep because when she next opened her eyes, she saw daylight streaming through a distant window in their building. She looked for her partners and saw them some distance away sitting and chatting in low voices.

She walked over to them and asked "Which way to the toilet? After I'm done, point me toward the water and I'll refill the tank to make it flush."

"We thought you had a hard and dangerous night, so we've done it for you. There's water in the tank and you'll find a bucket next to it so you can refill it," Jason said.

"Thanks, I appreciate that." She of course could have teleported to her condo's bathroom and been back before anyone noticed her absence. "When is our phone call with Sheila?"

Antonio looked at his watch and said, "We have about two more hours. Maybe you'll want something to eat and drink after you finish in the bathroom?"

Michelle nodded and headed toward the bathroom to take care of nature. She joined the men in their circle when she finished, pulling out a protein bar and water from her backpack. She had to be careful with what she said as she had advance knowledge from her conversation with Sheila. While she was grateful for the help of Antonio and Enrique, she would be glad when Jason was her only partner so she wouldn't have to guard her words and actions so much.

"I wonder what's going on with the drug factory. They have two security guards conked on the head, a power failure, a missing plant, and who knows what else. Surely, they are on alert and potentially looking for us bad actors?" Michelle said.

"We should be secure here. We found this place in darkness and none of us have been out in the daylight. If someone is looking for any of us based on our descriptions, they have a lot of ground to search. This region has over a million people in it, or did at one time," Antonio said.

"Enrique, did the guard get a close look at your face when he tried to take you into custody?" Michelle asked.

"If he did, I look like any other South American man. It's one of the reasons the CIA assigned me to Colombia as I look and speak like one of their citizens."

"Have you noticed the difference between Colombian and Venezuelan Spanish?" Jason asked Enrique.

"I'm a second-generation American and I learned Spanish at school, though I have some relatives from Mexico which allowed me to practice the language. The Spanish that you hear in Bogota is different from what I heard in Caracas and certainly different from Mexico. I didn't speak much of anything to the guard. There were not enough words for him to determine that I was from a different part of the Spanish-speaking world. He could describe my height, maybe my age, but it was too dark. I certainly couldn't identify him in a police lineup because of the poor lighting. I don't know if I had bad luck running into him, or if I was caught on video.

"If any of us were caught on video, they potentially know there are three men and a woman. If they are suspicious, they would ask around at hotels for anybody fitting our description and they would get an answer quickly if the hotel we stayed at plays the game with the corrupt government. That said, there's a lot of land and buildings in this region for them to find where we're hiding. It sounds like Sheila wants us to move out soon. So, our danger will be moving from this building to wherever a small plane is going to pick us up."

"What kind of work have you done for the agency in Colombia?" Michelle asked.

"I would tell you, but then I'd have to kill you. You know we're not supposed to talk about our work even to fellow case officers."

"Have you potentially been on the run from corrupt government authorities in Colombia in prior assignments? That's vague enough, isn't it?"

"The agency focuses on cocaine production and trafficking and FARC, which is an extremist group. I can't say that I have or haven't been involved in any of those topics."

They stopped talking and listened for a moment, hearing gravel crunch close to the building. When they had chosen this building to temporarily house them, the first thing they looked for was a hidey-hole in case someone came into the building. The four operatives now scattered to those locations and waited to see what would happen next.

The door opened and two men walked in. The four operatives were too far away initially to hear what the men were saying. As they walked around looking at the building, it became apparent that one of the men was a business owner while the other was a real estate agent. Fortunately, they didn't look in the bathroom which would've shown its recent occupation. They talked ameni-ties and monthly lease rates and then they left.

After the four of them reconvened, Michelle said, "That could've been a piece of bad luck if we had been caught squatting here."

"Did you hear what they were talking about? How good is your Spanish?" Antonio asked.

"I thought they were talking about leasing the building to start a new business. Apparently, my Spanish is very good, although I was some distance from their voices."

"Yeah, the business they want to open is an expansion of that plant we were trying to break into last night. He said he wanted to use the building as a plant nursery. I can't think of any need by the people of Ciudad Guayana to buy plants for landscaping. The only plant I can see them acquiring is the jimson weed plant."

"Did anyone get a picture of the two men? It's good to know who the enemy is," Jason asked. "They weren't in my sightline."

"I did, but it's an overhead shot, so it's not a good picture of their faces," Enrique said, showing them a few pictures on his phone.

"I was so busy concentrating on staying hidden and trying to catch their conversation, I didn't even think to use my camera. I'll get better at this, gentlemen."

"Well, it's another event to add to our discussion with Sheila. It's not good that they're trying to expand their production. That means that someone is paying for an expansion and there's a busi-ness plan somewhere that shows what kind of profits they can make with this plant," Antonio said. "I've seen this plan before in Colombia. Farmers are convinced to give up growing agriculture crops and replace them with coca plants."

# CHAPTER 19

 $\mathcal{M}$ ichelle stayed on the lookout while the other three conversed with Sheila. Normally, they all spoke with her, but after the surprise of the real estate agent, they were afraid they might not hear the approach of a car over the sound of their voices. She was fairly sure she'd been thoroughly briefed earlier by Sheila. If not, the guys would brief her. She found an area up high with a window that she could look out of. She waited till the guys' backs were turned, and she teleported up onto a beam. They were impressed with her upper arm strength for getting up that high.

Sheila briefed them on the Seal team that had been dispatched by a naval ship in the Caribbean and had been on the Orinoco River since yesterday heading toward their present coordinates. Sheila expected that Michelle would brief the Seal team on the interior of the factory and then she would join the other three waiting near a small airport to move on in a small plane to one of the other three cities on Sheila's list. The Seals were expected to arrive in about three hours. As they were a striking group of men, they would be unable to leave their boat in full daylight and not be noticed. Especially considering the duffel bag full of explosives they were carrying. They would be pulling the boat ashore upriver of the dock that the drug factory was using. They would wait till dark and move in to blow the business up. The agents ended their conversation with Sheila and just stayed on watch for any strangers to approach the building. They would all leave once darkness arrived, but Michelle would be going in a different direction. As soon as she was out of eyesight of her three teammates, she teleported to the river to look for the American Seals.

Since she didn't want to die, she texted Sheila to relay to the team that she was close by and not to shoot. She gave Sheila a few minutes for that message to transport itself back and forth between the United States and Venezuela and through a few satellites along the way. Then she advanced forward to where she believed the men were waiting.

They abruptly appeared before her, which scared the wits out of her. Once her wits were back in her head and her tongue back in her mouth, she gave a faint "Hi, I'm Michelle Watson."

"Ma'am, I understand you've been inside our target building and will brief us. Here's a piece of paper to draw what you saw. If you can remember where people and exits were located, please add them to the paper."

Michelle did so, including warning them where she'd seen the workers wearing safety gear. She wouldn't want this Seal team to be showered with fentanyl powder after the building exploded. She walked them through her drawing and what people were armed with inside the building. She prepared them with as much detail as she could. They were ready for her to leave and do some more planning themselves. She asked the leader, "Would you text me that you're all safe? Once I hear the building explode from the other end of town, I'm moving on to another city to explore another potential drug-making facility. I suspect you and your men will follow me there. Good luck, men." Michelle gave them a wave as she left to go join her team.

She was meeting up with her teammates across the river at a

small airfield. She would teleport there and beat them to the landing field. She would of course tell them that the Seal team gave her a ride across the river. Only Jason would know the truth. She was sitting on the ground and texted her three teammates about her arrival. She had a view across the river of approximately where the drug factory was located. She kept looking for fireworks in the distance but saw nothing. Finally, there was an earth-shaking kaboom. It was like watching Beethoven's Fifth Symphony set to fireworks; there was a rhythm to the explosions. She hoped that all who wanted to leave got out.

Perhaps an hour later, the remainder of her team arrived at the airfield. They waited for a few minutes as a small plane landed. They quickly boarded and headed for the west for the other three cities they needed to explore.

Michelle asked, "Did you see the explosion?"

"You bet. That was well done. Are they following us to the next location?" Jason asked.

"I don't know. I was just happy to see that factory destroyed and for us to be safely out of there. The Seals seemed a little more vulnerable to being caught. You would think that the military or the police force would swarm that explosion site. But the Seal team came in by boat down the river and maybe they're getting out of there in a different small plane than we did. I'm sure Sheila will keep us informed. Does the pilot know where we're going?" Michelle asked.

"I hear we're heading for Valencia. The analysts must've seen something on satellite to interest them in that city. It's also the next largest city after Caracas that's closest to our present location, so maybe Sheila just has us working westward," Jason said.

"Well, my friends, we may as well catch some sleep. It's cooler in the plane than likely our future digs will be in the next city," Antonio said. "Of course, it would be nice if we were flying lower, but there are some mountains between us and Valencia and we don't want to hit them in the dark."

With those words of advice, they were all soon leaning against the wall of the plane to try to get comfortable and sleep. The pilot woke them as he was descending.

"I've been informed that Venezuela has launched a jet that is heading our way. I'm going to try and land. It's better than being shot out of the sky."

"Let us know if we can help," Enrique said.

None of them wanted to distract the pilot. Michelle thought briefly of her two kids back in California. If they crashed in this plane, would her body ever be found? She promised herself that if the plane was heading for a crash, she would teleport somewhere and not die. Fortunately, Sheila had found a phenomenal pilot who was able to safely bring the plane down in the dark and not hit anything.

"Should we try to cover the wings, so the light doesn't reflect off the metal?" Michelle asked.

"The plane is painted a flat black; it doesn't show at night. We're good. I would love to get closer to the forest, but I don't want to waste gas as we'll eventually need to fly somewhere."

"Do you have any rocket-propelled weapons?" Michelle asked.

"No. Not a good idea; that would be like waving a red flag at a bull. Besides, the plane is moving fast and unless they're close to the launcher and heat-seeker, you'd have a tiny chance of hitting their plane. Let's just sit quietly and hope they don't have thermal-imaging technology in their plane. We're dead meat if they do," said the pilot.

They heard the jet stream past overhead which was good news.

"How long should we sit here before getting back in the air?" Jason asked.

"I would guess at least an hour. There are small planes such as this one that smuggle drugs so they don't want to randomly blow small planes out of the sky as the country will lose money and anger their Colombian partners. I have more technology on my small plane to sense stuff, plus the agency moved a satellite to focus on this part of the world. We should be able to get some help from the sky."

"How many planes are there?" Michelle asked.

"The good news is the Venezuelan military has only nineteen planes at our last count. It is hard to keep just nineteen planes in the air with maintenance, parts, and pilot training. Each plane is different and some date as far back as the 1950s. So that plane isn't going to be very good at looking for us, and there is only one of them."

"Can you tell where it is now?"

"Yes. It is over one hundred miles away. It appears to be the only plane they launched. The military has a few helicopters and two or three fighter jets, but it all depends on where they were parked when they were launched. Ideally, we would find another small plane and try to follow that to Valencia, but that's not the usual drug-running route."

Enrique asked, "Would it make sense to go farther south before heading north to Valencia?"

"That probably wouldn't be noticed. I don't know that they have active radar in all parts of this country. Remember, the country is in shambles and they haven't been able to keep up with their infrastructure. If I were El Presidente, I wouldn't waste money and resources on having the radar active and monitored any more than I needed to keep commercial jets in the air."

They nodded at that decision-making process. Still, El Presidente had made many bad decisions to drag the country down to where it was now.

"I think it's clear to go. Does anyone need to use the great outhouse out there before we take off?"

"I do," Michelle said, opening the door to scramble out. She hadn't thought about it until the pilot asked the question, but the mind-numbing vibration of the small plane was enough to make anyone want to pee.

After she returned to the plane, the four men got out, apparently also affected by the vibration. Soon they were underway again, and the rest of their journey was uneventful. It was just as the pilot said—the jet fighter was going fast with limited technology and training. It couldn't find their small plane.

Michelle was curious about the pilot. He was obviously an American and the little plane was outfitted to hide from any authorities. So when he wasn't helping move them around Venezuela, where were he and his plane parked? Maybe he was stationed in Colombia, which had a slightly better relationship with the United States. She wondered if there was another, larger plane just like this plane to move the Seal team around the country. They were on the Orinoco River which didn't flow toward Valencia, and she couldn't see them taking another couple of days to go up the river by boat and into the Caribbean Sea and to the naval ship that dispatched them. On the other hand, it would take Michelle and her group a few days to find a new drug facility in Valencia, so why not go back to their ship? Or maybe the ship had a few teams to dispatch and while waiting for the first team to return, there was a second team on its way to a new target.

On that thought, she returned to sleep and didn't awaken again until the pilot notified all of them that he would be landing for fuel. That was the disadvantage of a plane like this. Clearly, it had been modified in many ways. But there were physics involved in weight, wingspan, and engine size. They were soon back in the air and Michelle briefly thought of how the pilot knew where he could find fuel in a country that didn't have much of it. Before she could reason an answer to that question, she was back asleep.

As dawn was showing itself, Michelle could see the tall buildings denoting a bigger city in Venezuela. She asked the pilot if this was Valencia, and he nodded. It was a big city, near a lake and surrounded by mountains. It was still hot in this part of Venezuela. After this case was over, she was going to visit somewhere cold like Iceland. She would sleep well in an ice hotel and gaze at the stars. The image was so vivid that she shivered for a moment before an air current rocked the plane, reminding her she was in stifling heat. It was nice to have an aerial view of the city before their pilot put the small plane down on a dirt road in an agriculture field. They got out and their plane taxied and lifted off for parts unknown.

"Okay, where to?" Michelle asked. It was a funny question to ask given that she could teleport to anywhere on earth at a moment's notice, but she was locked here because Antonio and Enrique didn't know about her special skill.

"Let's call the boss and find out where she wants us to head. In a city with over a million people, we have too many choices. We need her to narrow it down, so we're close to whatever drug production building she has in mind," Jason said.

They stepped inside a group of trees, so they weren't in anyone's sightline, and dialed Langley, Virginia.

"I see you made it to Valencia without incident."

"I don't know about that. We had a fighter jet come after our small plane. But according to our pilot, it was only one of two jet fighter planes that they own, and it might have been manufactured in the 1950s. We kinda like those odds," Michelle said.

"I could have an analyst look up the statistics of how many planes have been shot down over Venezuela in the last twenty years. I suspect you're in greater danger from being shot at from the ground than having a plane shoot you down," Sheila said.

"I have positive thoughts of the encounter with the jet fighter; let's not wreck those positive feelings with actual facts."

"Okay, Boss, now that you know we're all alive, where do you want us to go? Have the analysts pinpointed an area that might be used for drug production?" Jason asked.

"We studied the industrial areas much like the last location. There isn't a major river, and the lake really doesn't serve transportation needs. The railways are working. So to move product from the production site to out of the country, in the case of

Valencia it makes sense to be near the airport. There's an industrial area just north of the airport which at one time contained a great number of American companies. There was an assembly plant for Ford Motor Company, a Coca-Cola plant, etc.; we're running down a few buildings in that area. What we'd like you to do right now is to find a vacant building to be your new base in that area. Why don't you try the Ford Motor Company assembly plant as it ceased operations about four years ago? There should be many places to hide inside there."

"Was there any fallout that you've heard through diplomatic channels about the explosion in Ciudad Guayana?" Antonio asked.

"Understand that when anything bad happens in that country, Maduro blames the West and in particular the United States. This time he just happens to be right."

"And the Seal team, they got away safely?" Michelle asked.

"They did. Anything else?"

They ended the call soon after that and started walking. Their phone GPS pointed them toward the assembly plant, but it helped that it was located on Henry Ford Avenue. There weren't a lot of people walking around and they were conspicuous as a group of four, so they split up as best they could and headed toward their destination. When they got there eventually, it was surrounded by a cyclone fence with barbed wire.

"Do you think there is security on the inside, or is the building just abandoned?" Michelle asked.

"Most of the businesses had a good decade of decline under Chavez before Maduro took over. I would think that any wise American business would have removed expensive assets before they shut it down. And if there are no expensive assets, there's no need for security. The fence is probably there just to keep squatters out."

"Should we walk the perimeter and look for an easy way in?" Jason asked.

Michelle looked at the heavy chain and lock keeping the gate closed and said, "I'm really good at climbing fences and picking locks. Why don't you guys turn back toward the road and make sure no one's around watching and I'll take care of this for us."

Antonio and Enrique looked skeptically at Michelle, so Jason said, "Trust me guys, she has a strange set of skills. She'll have us inside in no time. Let's turn around and watch the road just to make sure no one's watching us. We'll have to scatter if we see a police or military presence."

The moment that she saw Antonio and Enrique turn their backs, she teleported to the other side of the fence. She shook the fencing a little to make a noise like she was climbing it, then said "I'm in. Give me a moment on this lock."

They both glanced over their shoulders at her, startled that she had navigated the three rows of barbed wire at the top so quickly. She had learned to pick locks during her time at the police academy. She found it relaxing and as a street cop had to use the skill to break into a few residences. She was opening the gates for them in no time. Once they were inside; they closed the gates and locked the chains, and then hustled toward the building. Michelle had a little more difficulty there because someone had locked the doors from the inside with chains. Simply picking the lock didn't get them inside.

"Whoever wisely locked up this assembly plant in this manner had to lock the final door in the regular way with a key to get out of there. How about if I climb up on the roof and find a stairwell to go down and then come open this door for you? You guys can stay tucked out of sight to anyone walking by on the street, given the shape of this entrance."

As no one had a better idea, Michelle hurried out of sight and then up to the roof. She found the door and teleported inside of the building. It had been locked in the same manner as the front door. She decided she had better take the chain and lock off the door to make her story believable. She picked the lock and removed the chain, planning to relock it before they left the building for the final time. No need to let squatters destroy the inside of the building.

She arrived at the front door and picked the inside lock and opened the door to let her teammates inside.

"Let's explore this building. Maybe there's a comfortable place to sleep. Maybe they left behind foam from the upholstery shop. We also need water. It is unlikely that a single faucet inside this plant works, or if it does, is the water safe?" Jason said.

When they set off exploring, Michelle thought about getting one of those five-gallon jugs of water that sit atop water coolers and bringing it back here like it had been left behind at the time of the plant's closure. However, she could only teleport herself or something like a backpack. Still, she could make a run on her pantry and come back with six to eight bottles of water on each teleportation trip. It would be an American bottle of water and might raise suspicions from their partners. If things got desperate, she would at least transport one-gallon jugs of water. She pulled out her cell phone to see if it was due to rain soon. They could at least collect rainwater. That didn't look promising. She texted Sheila with their problem and asked if there was an unopened five-gallon jug that she could teleport to Venezuela. She was pleased when she was notified to be in her office in five minutes. She wasn't sure how she was going to get it back as anything she had teleported in the past was in a large duffel bag or backpack. Given the weight of this jug, she would have to hug it tightly to her chest. Would that still teleport with her? She decided to do a simple experiment. She took her backpack off and wrapped it tightly in her arms in the front and then teleported across the factory. She was pleasantly surprised that it went with her. She was still trying to understand these teleport properties.

On schedule, she appeared in Sheila's office. The unopened five-gallon bottle stood on her desk. Michelle gathered it up to take it back with her to Valencia. Before she departed, she told

Sheila to make sure that the next Seal team brought water with them for her team. She had a good cover story to get one jug to Venezuela, but she could think of no story to get a second jug to her team.

She was excited when in a moment later she stood inside an office in the closed Ford Motor Company assembly plant holding the heavy jug. Not only was she ecstatic about finding water for the team, but she was also thrilled with this new aspect of her teleportation skill.

She texted the others and said she found a five-gallon unopened jug in one of the offices, giving them directions on where to find her. They were soon slaking their thirst.

"I thought Colombia was a rough assignment, but Venezuela is so much worse. We never had trouble finding water. Perhaps it was where we were stationed, but they have more infrastructure there. I guess that is why so many people are fleeing this country for Colombia."

# CHAPTER 20

They spent the remainder of the day looking for water. They found some dirty water in various places, and it was enough to make the toilet flush and Michelle was happy. She of course could have teleported home to use the toilet, but that felt like cheating. They did find some foam in the upholstery area. It was enough for a pillow but not a bed. Their large bottle of water was emptying quickly, and Michelle wished she'd grabbed three or four bottles. The good news was they had not explored every nook and cranny of the assembly plant. Michelle was sure she could plant additional bottles for the other men to find. She sent a text to Sheila asking her to line up an additional three bottles. She moved bottles into places and then threw dirt on them so they looked like they had been sitting there for four years. She was worried about their food supply so when she figured out what everyone was eating in terms of protein bars or MREs, she fetched that from Virginia and restocked their backpacks.

She'd had to hide her smile when Antonio said that there appeared to be a food fairy who kept restocking his backpack. Enrique agreed, as did Jason, but he knew that she was the food fairy who was restocking their supplies. Life would be so much easier if she could just admit to her teleporting talent. The good thing was she could disappear in the car assembly plant and no one wondered where she disappeared to, as they all searched the large facility for useful items and to relieve their boredom. It was a safe and quiet place to wait for their next instructions from Langley.

The next day they finally had a call from Sheila with instructions on where the next drug factory potentially was located. The good news was they didn't have to go far. There was a Quaker facility that had closed four years prior. Satellite imagery again showed heat and light around the clock in the building with shipments coming and going. The facility was about three blocks away. The only problem with their current digs was they hadn't found a way to come and go with ease. No one else had Michelle's lock-picking skills and they worried about leaving the locks open. Michelle found an old combination lock on an empty toolbox in the assembly plant and cracked the numbers, so they all had a way to leave and return through the one entrance while keeping the place locked up.

Sheila sent the aerial photos and the group discussed the layout compared to the drug factory in Ciudad Guayana. They made a guess on how it was laid out, then discussed a plan.

"I'm the best at scaling fences quickly and gaining access. Why don't you three stay here, while I go about surveillance tonight?" Michelle said.

"Actually, Antonio and I were talking about how little help we've been on this mission. We both have experience with explosives and rather than moving in a Seal team, perhaps the CIA should send us in to take down these buildings."

"I can't comment on that as I know nothing about explosives. Do you have some explosives in your backpacks that you can use to blow up the building?" Michelle asked.

"We don't. But if the CIA can have that pilot fly us around this country, then he could bring the explosives to us. I think it's dangerous using the US military to blow the sites up. It sets up an awkwardness for the United States in the eyes of the rest of the world even though we're doing the right thing by taking a drug off the market that would do damage not only to our country but to the other countries as well. However, Venezuela would report that innocent citizens died in these factories."

"I'd ask you how you would blow that building up, but I don't understand enough about explosives to know if your idea would work. I have no skin in the game as to who blows up the buildings. I also don't have the expertise to determine who's the best at blowing them up. Why don't you give Sheila a call? You'll need her help to get the explosives here, so she's the one you have to convince, not myself or Michelle," Jason said.

Antonio took that to heart and made the call. Sheila agreed with the request, and he sent a list of supplies. They had a quiet overnight in the factory, while the CIA made arrangements to deliver the explosives. The next day, Antonio and Enrique were out picking up their supplies from a delivery from their little flat-black painted plane, Jason and Michelle were in the factory doing a daily workout. Michelle hated working up a sweat when there wasn't a shower nearby, but at least they had baby wipes to wipe the worst of the body odor. Michelle's phone rang and it was Sheila.

"I've been thinking about you being able to move five-gallon bottles of water. I'd like you to try an experiment. Would you hug Jason tightly and see if you can move him around the building?"

"Ah, I don't understand how my magic works, but what if Jason's torso comes with me as that is what is touching my body, but his legs stay behind?"

Jason looked up in alarm upon hearing Michelle's side of the conversation. She put the call on speaker.

"Sheila, I've just put the call on speaker so Jason can hear what we're talking about. He looks alarmed with my explanation."

"Okay, I get your point. Can you try an inanimate object that is human-sized—is there something that is six-foot-tall that you could practice with? Maybe with Jason, you have to twine your legs around his and wrap your arms around his head. You get my suggestion. Try doing that with something lying around the factory."

"Okay," Michelle said with dubiousness in her voice. At least it was safer to try that before practicing on a human. They ended their call as Michelle started looking for an object.

"Okay, what's up? Why does Sheila think you might be able to teleport me?"

"So, you know those five-gallon jugs of water we have seen around the factory?"

Jason nodded and replied, "I assume you teleported them here in a duffle bag."

"Actually, I hugged the jug to my chest and it got here with me."

Suddenly, Jason understood what Sheila was asking and what Michelle's fears were, but he was very excited at the notion. If Michelle could get the two of them out of danger, they would be far more effective spies for the agency, and they were already great spies.

"Ah, I understand. Let's find some objects of different shapes and experiment and then you can try me."

"No. I'm not trying to teleport with you as my first human experiment. Let the agency find some comatose prisoner some-where and I'll crawl into bed with them and see if I can move them. That way if I cause any physical harm, it's not the end of the world."

Michelle spent thirty minutes experimenting with various objects, and it did indeed seem that if she wasn't hugging a longer object from tip to bottom, it simply didn't move with her. Jason watched all the experiments, and then they were on the phone again with Sheila asking for her to find the perfect prisoner to experiment upon.

Antonio and Enrique returned with full and heavy duffle bags. Michelle would be breaking into the building after dark to get a picture of the drug factory layout. In the interim, they set about putting things together so that they would be ready to bring down the building that night. Michelle, as the team member who climbed fences and walls easily, would do the work of placing explosives in high places.

Sheila sent her a text telling her that once she was done exploring the old Quaker food factory building, she located the perfect human to experiment upon. Michelle had a busy night ahead of her. She vowed that after her experiment with the comatose prisoner, she would make a quick stop at her condominium to take a real shower. She would need it after the heat of Venezuela and the yuckiness of tightly hugging a comatose human who was a stranger.

Finally, it was dark, and Michelle left the Ford plant to walk to the old cereal factory. Of course, the moment she was out of the eyesight of their two CIA agents, she was outside the fence around that factory, and then she was on the roof. Just like the car factory, the cereal factory had a stairwell from the roof to whatever was going on below. She then teleported around the old cereal complex and mapped it out. She returned to the roof to waste about half an hour so her fellow agents wouldn't wonder how she could map out a complex so quickly. She didn't want them to lack confidence in it. She moved from the roof of the cereal factory to the roof of the car factory and then to just inside the front door. She walked slowly to the far end of the deserted assembly plant to join the rest of her team. She jogged the last few steps just before she came into view so that she would look like she ran the entire time she was gone.

She pretended to catch her breath and said, "Where's the pen and paper?"

She drew out the factory from memory, then showed the two explosives experts. They chatted acronyms that meant nothing to Michelle. She only reminded them that she could plant stuff up high. Their discussion went back and forth for a while and then they had their plan. They needed some time to assemble the explosives but were confident the explosives could be deployed before dawn. All four of them would place different explosives in different parts of the building. Michelle would leave some on the inside. She had seen a place in the rafters that was perfect.

Antonio assured Michelle and Jason that there would be a timer that wouldn't go off until all four were back together and safe. In fact, Antonio wanted to set it off from the roof of the car assembly plant so they could all watch. Their planting of explosives went as planned and they all followed Michelle up the stairwell in the car plant to the roof. After they were seated and looking toward the cereal factory, Antonio began setting charges off.

"This is going to accidentally kill some people inside who just want a job paying a wage in a poor country," Michelle said.

"They're making the drug which will kill innocent people around the world as it's highly addictive and organ damaging. This is not the way for the country to get back on its feet economically. I don't feel very bad about the people who will die. Besides, unless they're next to the explosives, they'll likely survive. They might have a piece of roof or wall fall on them, but it won't kill them. The buildings look fragile in this country, and they are single stories," Enriquez said. "It's a good thing you don't work in the agency in Colombia—there are innocents there who die all the time for no other reason than they have sought employment in the drug cartels."

Michelle nodded and Antonio hit the button to begin the explosions. At first, nothing happened and just when their minds tricked them into thinking they had made a mistake, the night sky lit up with light and sound. Not long after that, they heard sirens.

Some seemed to be building alarms; others were likely first responders.

"Well, it is time to move on to a new city. Where is our man in the black plane?" Enrique asked.

"He's waiting for us at the airport," Antonio said, looking at his phone. "We just received a text from Langley. It's time to move."

They watched the activity of the first responders for a few moments and decided to beat it out of town quickly. Michelle locked up the building and the fence and they were four people in a hurry to reach the airport, which was a mere quarter mile away. They split up into twosomes and hurried as fast they could without trying to look guilty of something. Which they were.

They managed to reach the plane and get into the air while flames were still shooting from the building. The pilot set the plane down about halfway between Valencia and their next destination in case there was another military jet in the air or indeed any other plane looking for them.

The Americans had on their side sneakiness and fuel. The Venezuelans were lacking planes, fuel, and pilots, and it would take them some time to get into the air. Their next target, Barquisimeto, was about one-hundred-forty miles away. In another thirty minutes, they would arrive at their destination. Their pilot watched his instruments for a while and then said, "Here it comes."

They heard the roar of a loud plane overhead, but it was too little too late to catch them. It eventually circled back on the other side of the valley that they were parked in. Their pilot said it was time to move, and he stayed low over the mountains between the two major cities.

"I need you folks ready to bail out as soon as we land. I'm choosing to land in a train yard as it's not well used anymore, and the landing is open and flat. It's closer to the industrial park. This way we avoid the airport which has only one plane arriving and departing each day. In a city of nearly a million people, the need for only one flight per day says something about how bad the economy is."

Indeed, thought his occupants, as they tried to imagine a city of a million inhabitants with a single commercial jet landing each day. Michelle moved on to worry about water again. They would find somewhere to stay and go from there.

They moved through the rail yard and into another industrial park. Michelle noticed the ubiquitous blue plastic barrels on the roofs and knew this was another city without water. The barrels collected rainwater and fed the water inside to apartments. What a sad situation. Dawn was upon them, and it became harder to tell which businesses were closed overnight and which were closed forever. Eventually, they found a warehouse to borrow for their living quarters and settled in with a little help from Michelle's lock-picking and fence-scaling skills.

They began exploring the building and Michelle managed to take Jason aside to let him know she needed to disappear for an hour. He said he would cover for her and that she should teleport outside the factory, and he would let her know where she should come inside. She nodded and texted Sheila to find out where she should meet her. Though Michelle was thousands of miles away, she would get to the location sooner than Sheila. There was a candidate for the teleportation experiment whom Sheila found close by, so she had Michelle meet her in the CIA parking lot for a short drive to the facility.

Indeed, there was a prison hospital that had a younger man injured in a prison fight with no family. The CIA brought a second bed into the room to see if Michelle could transport him from one bed to the next. It was so awkward. First, she tried wrapping herself around the man—she had one arm around his torso, and another around his head and she wrapped both legs around his. Just she and Sheila were in the room; otherwise, she thought she might die of embarrassment from hugging a complete stranger who was so obviously not there. A moment later they were in the second bed. She tried it again just hugging the man around his torso with both hands. This time she moved, but he didn't. She was relieved that his body stayed whole and that she hadn't teleported just a piece of a human. So, it appeared that the key to her teleportation skill was that she had to wrap herself around another human or object to bring it with her. This was groundbreaking. She would practice the skill with Jason, but now she could rescue him. She felt the thrill of new achievement. Now she just wanted to head home for a quick shower before returning return to Venezuela.

# CHAPTER 21

$\mathcal{M}$ichelle did as planned, stopping for a quick shower only to put her dirty clothes back on. Then she was back at the factory, texting Jason. He told her where to teleport inside and she resumed searching the facility despite the fact she'd been gone forty minutes. She saw Jason approaching her.

"Tell me what you learned."

"We'll have to try teleporting at some point, but if I just hug you like a normal human hug, you remain behind but whole. If I wrap my legs around yours, put one arm around your torso and the other to your head in a tight hug, I think you'll be able to come with me."

"Wow. Let's try it now."

"Where are Antonio and Enrique?"

"They are on the hunt for water."

"You're sure they won't come this way?"

"Yeah, water is going to be a problem in each Venezuelan city that we visit," Jason said.

"Let me think of a solution without revealing my talent."

"Okay, hug me tight, and let's see if we can move to the far side of the room."

As Michelle got closer, Jason sniffed her and said, "You smell good. You must have grabbed a shower while you were in Virginia."

"I had to. I don't like hugging comatose men," she said wrinkling her nose. "I put my dirty clothes back on, though."

A moment later they tipped and fell over, as Michelle tightly held onto Jason, thus over-balancing him, but they moved across the room before they fell.

"That's so cool! Okay, take me to the auto assembly plant in Valencia."

"I need to figure out how to not overbalance first. We might crack our heads if we move and then crash to the concrete. I'm going to use one leg to be a tripod, and I'll use the other leg to wrap around you. Let's see if that works."

Michelle was pleased to see that worked as they didn't go tumbling to the ground.

"Okay, now let me see if I can grab you quickly and move you."

Michelle sped up her pace, wrapped herself around Jason, and before he knew what hit him, he was standing in the auto factory building.

"Wow! Wow! You were the best partner ever before; now I can't think of words to describe you. If you had discovered this during the last case, we could have coshed that woman on her head instead of fetching kayaks. You could take me back to Maryland for a shower even."

"Speaking of teleporting, let's get back to Barquisimeto before the others return."

Michelle moved them as instructed. Once they returned to the factory, Michelle's phone rang, and the ID said it was Sheila.

"Have you practiced moving Jason around?"

"Yes. I've been successful. I just moved us to Valencia and back."

"I've been thinking about this case. I think we need to teleport the botanist who created this plant to the United States. I think you're the avenue of how we get him here."

"Why?" Jason asked.

"I could leave you guys in Venezuela, and you'll be playing whack-a-mole. We can blow up their facilities and they can keep re-creating the plant."

"True. The way to prevent that is to have him in custody on American soil," Jason said as the idea took root.

"Now we don't know who he or she is, or where they're located, but we'll figure that out in the next few days. Then you can bring them to my office."

"Ah, Boss, won't that create all kinds of questions within the agency? Like, how did they reach Langley?"

"Yes, but the truth is beyond everyone's imagination. It will add to my mystique."

"Okay then," Michelle said with a laugh. "Then, what is our mission here at the moment? Do we continue to find these drug factories and destroy them? Do you want to give Antonio and Enrique new explosives to destroy the remaining drug factories and put us on the tail of the botanist?"

"I haven't figured that out yet. There's no need to split you up until I have a reading on the botanist."

"How will you find the botanist?" Michelle asked, curious about searching for a scientist in a country of twenty-eight million.

"I don't pretend to understand the science involved here. I believe they can determine the geography of where the plant was grown by the soil and roots."

"What happens if your data says Ciudad Guayana? Does that necessarily mean the botanist is there?"

"Let's hope it says more than that."

They ended the call shortly after that.

"Okay, back to our current problems: We need water. Should

we tap into one of these blue barrels on the rooftops? We have water sterilization tablets."

"I'd rather steal bottled water from my condo."

"Yeah, but why is water just lying around here?"

"How about we say we found it in a nearby building?" Jason suggested.

"Okay, but how do we get rid of the English labels?"

"Can we just take the labels off? We'll still see that the bottles are sealed."

"Okay, where are your bottles? I'll fetch them and you can de-label them."

He described where they were and where she could find a razor blade to aid his removal of the labels, and in under ten minutes, they were set for water for their team. Jason texted Antonio and Enrique that he found water and they could return. They said they would be back in fifteen minutes.

"If it's going to take that long, I'll grab some more water. The warehouse store in California hasn't opened yet. I'll leave them a ten-dollar bill and grab a case. Be back in a sec," and she was. They swiftly removed the labels and had quite a water cache.

With the water problem solved, they returned to discussing their plans for the next building explosion and the move to the final city, Maracaibo. Antonio and Enrique were admittedly puzzled by the water cache but had no reason other than the one supplied by Jason for its presence. When they were transported by the plane, the pilot had supplied them with a couple days' food. This building, like the previous warehouses, had bathrooms, and they found sufficient water in the pipes that, while undrinkable, was flushable. With their basic needs taken care of, they settled in to play cards and wait for information from the agency on where their target might be in the city of Barquisimeto. Their next call with Sheila came after two days of waiting.

"The Venezuelans have seen a pattern to the buildings set on fire. They stopped activity in the building in Barquisimeto. We had to go back and look at historic satellite feeds to find the possible production site. This one is about ten miles away on the southwest side of the city. It is a large box store that had to close once Venezuela started suffering food shortages. It's in the middle of a residential area, so it can be hard to find a place to hide near it, and we have our pilot looking at where he can pick you up that is close by. Michelle, we will likely send you ahead to verify the factory's purpose and then maybe we can get in there and destroy it before they return workers to the site. I wanted you to know our plans and I'll call you back when they're a little firmer."

Sheila left them the address of the warehouse so they could study the area around it and discuss their approach. About a quarter-mile away was some vacant land dotted by a few houses. Perhaps at one point it had been a farm. They suggested the location to Sheila to see if the pilot could land there.

They enlarged other parts of the picture and pointed to a collection of automobiles. They couldn't tell from the satellite photos if it was a junkyard or a closed car rental agency. Regardless, Michelle would check out the cars after she was done with the building. They were fortunate that in this city, the bus system still worked. The plan was for Michelle to take the last bus of the day which was late afternoon. She would have a walk of perhaps half a mile and then she could check out the two locations.

"Michelle, I could go with you and hotwire a car to get us there and back here," Antonio said.

"That's not a bad idea. I think, though, it would be better if I scout the two areas, then text you guys and you can hotwire a car to reach me. That would save me figuring out how to get back here and it would help us establish our new base. I'm not sure where you'll find a car that has gas in it. You only need a gallon to go that distance, and maybe we can find some here somewhere."

"Actually, that won't be a problem. When we were exploring earlier, we found a gas station that was open and had gas. We'll go get a gallon now, then I'll be ready to hotwire a car after dark and we'll join you."

The two set off and Jason said, "Since the guys will be gone for ten to fifteen minutes, you could teleport me to my condo so I can get a shower and grab a few chocolate bars."

"I could, but this part of my skill is really new to me and I'm not confident with it. If for some reason I couldn't get you back here, that would royally screw up the mission, and all for a shower and some chocolate."

"You're right. Once this mission is over, we'll have to test your skill so you have confidence in it. You should probably practice walking up behind me and trying to wrap me up so you can move me. I presume when we find the botanist that he or she won't willingly stand there while you hug them. I know my first reaction would be to throw you off."

"That's a good point. Even if I entered their house in the middle of the night and found them in bed. If I pounce on them enough to wrap my arms and legs around them, I'd probably get thrown off. I wonder how I should quickly subdue them?"

"Personally, since this is the inventor of a deadly and addictive drug, I would have no problem using chloroform or some injectable on them. You might be able to disable them enough with a hit to the head, but if you render them unconscious you might actually cause brain damage and I'm sure the CIA would like to interview this person. Besides how well can you move deadweight? Why don't you pose that question to Sheila and make her come up with a solution? If you're going to use chemical means, you'll need to fetch that from her."

"There's something to be said for pepper-spraying the botanist. The person they had me move in Virginia was dead weight, but I just moved him from soft bed to soft bed. I'm not sure what moving a person from wherever I find them to Sheila's office would leave me uninjured. That would cause some misery and they would be much easier to subdue if they're in pain from the pepper spray, but I'll pose the question to Sheila and see what the agency comes up with. I do have pepper spray on me, so I wouldn't have to go to Langley to pick it up."

Antonio and Enrique returned, carrying the standard red one-gallon jug of gasoline. In Venezuela, though it was probably a four-liter jug. They also brought back information on the cost of the bus ride and the change required. The less Michelle spoke Spanish, the less she would stand out to any civilian. She practiced any conversation she might need with Antonio for the bus driver and she was ready to go stand at the bus stop. She had a piece of cardboard to create shade as she had seen other Venezuelan women do in the hot South American sun. A bus pulled up to her stop, and fortunately, it was full, with standing room only. It was much easier to hide inside a crowd than be forced to deal with a bus driver as the lone passenger. She set her phone to vibrate when they were coming to the stop she wanted. Her walking would take her past the place with all the autos and the empty field just about the time dusk was setting in. She planned to teleport inside the yard with the autos. From there, she would teleport close to the warehouse in question.

The passengers had thinned out by the time the bus reached Michelle's stop. She was pleased that no one got off with her. It was a drag walking down a major street worrying about an attack coming from any angle. She reached the corner of a building, paused for a quick glance at what was around her, and teleported to the yard with the cars. It turned out to be a junkyard and she could see the metal-crushing machine at one end. The last thing any of them wanted was to take a nap in a back seat and wake up when a forklift picks up the car to put it in the metal crusher. Like so many businesses, she wondered if this was still in operation. She moved around the junkyard trying to determine if any of the cars had less than a few weeks of dirt on them. She decided to wait until dark and then check the office for evidence of recent activity. Despite the danger of the metal crusher, she thought it was a safe place for them to hang out for the next thirty-six hours or so. She looked at the various cars to determine which had upholstery for a comfortable rest. She figured out a good collection of four cars and sent a picture to the rest of her team of where to meet her. She looked at the exterior locks on the facility and picked one, leaving the chain in place but the lock in the unlocked position. There appeared to be no car or person traffic near the gate, so the guys could be dropped off there with the remaining water and hopefully, no one would notice. Antonio could abandon the hot-wired car closer to the city in hopes that the owner might recover it.

Having found safe digs, she began exploring the targeted building. She teleported down the street close to the target building. She saw no lights on or cars in the parking lot. That was typical of many locations in Venezuela as electricity was expensive and inconsistent. Sheila had said that it appeared the Venezuelans had shut down other factories to hide them. She should probably figure out if this was a drug-making factory before her team made the effort to move closer to it. The agency was rarely wrong, so she thought that they were just trying to hide the factory. She looked for a roof to enter from, but this was a smaller factory than the two other locations. She decided to try the front door. She pulled on it to walk in, but it was locked. Time to use her special power.

She quickly opened her eyes but could see nothing. For a few seconds, she doubted her eyes were open, it was so dark. She moved her hands up her face just to feel her eyelids to make sure they were open. She pulled out her phone and turned on the flashlight app. She looked around for a light switch and turned it on, but nothing happened. Maybe there was no electricity that day, maybe they were conserving electricity in certain parts of the city, maybe it was controlled by a timer, or maybe there was just another reason the lights didn't work. It made it more difficult to see around the factory. She also wondered about the plants. The other factories had had around-the-clock growing lights.

She paused and texted her teammates with her thoughts that this might not be the factory. Antonio had just been about to find a car to hotwire, but they were going to stay in place until they heard more from her. After five minutes of searching the building, she could find no evidence that it was a drug factory. She texted her team and Sheila with the information. Antonio offered to come to fetch her, but she heard on the bus that it was running late that night because of a festival in another town, so she would be able to take the bus back to where they were hanging out. Of course, that was a complete lie, and she sat alone in the dark building playing solitaire on her phone until a certain amount of time passed and she could teleport to just outside of their present location.

She walked inside to where the guys were seated and said, "That was a good lesson tonight. Don't give up your current digs until you are sure you found your target."

"At least in this location I won't have nightmares of waking up in a car that's been loaded into a metal-crushing machine," Jason said.

Antonio and Enrique murmured their agreement.

Sheila had no other location for them to look for that night. In fact, she might just send them on to the final city, Maracaibo, if the analysts did not come up with a location. It was close to midnight in Venezuela and Sheila would move them by dusk the next day, if she couldn't find a drug factory in Barquisimeto. Their little black plane would pick them up at the same place he dropped them off at—a closed railroad yard.

# CHAPTER 22

$S$heila had her team on the move late the next day. They were waiting in the railroad yard when the little plane approached. It stopped just long enough for them to get inside the plane and close the doors. Before they had reached a seated position in the plane, it was taxiing down the rail yard and was in the air.

"I'm impressed that you stay hidden, yet you seem to have plenty of gas for this plane, and I love the chocolate bars you have on board," Michelle said.

"I would tell you how I do it, but then I would have to kill you as it's a state secret."

She just smiled at him at his response.

"How far to Maracaibo?" Antonio asked.

"It's just over one-hundred-sixty miles or about an hour in this plane if I don't have to do any emergency landings."

"We didn't blow anything up this evening, so hopefully no Venezuelan air force jets."

"Fingers crossed," the pilot said. "This next city is larger than Barquisimeto. Their airport has six flights a day at the present. It is a city of like two and a half million people. There are many places I can land just outside of the city on dirt, and I think that will be a better plan. You'll have to walk farther, but it's safer for me."

"Got it. We'll figure it out. Maybe we can find a hotel this time as we're getting quite rank," Antonio said.

"It's another city with water shortages, so good luck with that," the pilot said.

The four of them were searching hotels on their phones and they found some with decent reviews from a few days ago. Better still, they had working pools. If they couldn't get a shower, a chlorinated pool wasn't a bad substitute.

"Does the bus system work in this city?" Enrique asked.

"They use cargo trucks to move people at a variety of fares. We'll see what we can find once we know where we're landing," Jason said.

They saw the city and their pilot scouted a dusty road for a landing and take-off. They had about a two-block walk to a major thoroughfare and then it was a matter of waving a driver down with money, which was fairly easy to do. Antonio gave the driver directions to a major hotel, and they were soon checking in at a four-star hotel.

"I don't care how much this hotel costs, I just need running water. Even Colombia isn't this bad," Antonio said.

"Our budget will afford it," Jason said. "Look at all of those free nights the agency has had."

They soon had two rooms rented, each with two queen beds. Michelle was looking forward to sleeping in a real bed instead of on top of auto upholstery. She would teleport home to her own shower while Jason used the one here in their hotel room. That would save the country and the hotel a precious couple of gallons of water on her behalf. She also dumped their dirty clothes and brought back clean clothes for herself and Jason.

"I'm glad that the agency doesn't regularly assign me to work out in the field or jungle or whatever you call it. I like sleeping on my own bed at night and being able to shower and to not have to search for water to slake my thirst," Michelle said. "In fact, I hope the agency never sends me back to this country."

"We haven't had operatives here for a while. The country is in such disarray politically that it can't cause trouble for the United States. I think you're safe in assuming you'll never be assigned here again. By the way, thanks for doing my laundry. If the guys ask us about our clean clothes, we did them in the shower and then ironed them dry. Just so our story is the same."

Michelle gave him a thumbs up and said, "What's on our agenda for the rest of the evening?"

"Unless Sheila calls with a target, I think we should settle in with a good book and go to bed early. I'm tired because I haven't been sleeping well on these hard surfaces."

"I couldn't agree more. I'll text the guys, tell them that we've ordered room service and are staying in tonight. They're probably as tired as we are and may choose to do the same thing. Do they have room service here?"

"I think if we offered to pay the hotel for their time, they would fetch whatever we need. It may not be cooked in the hotel's kitchen, but I would bet that they get food from somewhere."

"Okay, I'll try them first to see if we can get any food. I'd be happy with a peanut butter and jelly sandwich as I'm so tired of the MREs and protein bars," Michelle said. "I know I shouldn't complain as many agents spent time in the field in worse conditions, but this isn't what I joined the agency for."

She contacted the hotel to see what the availability of food was at the late hour. They would send her two traditional Maracaibo meals if she wanted. She agreed not knowing what would be delivered, but it would arrive in thirty minutes. She then texted the other two agents, who likewise liked the idea.

Their meal turned out to be a plantain sandwich stuffed with beef, cheese, lettuce, tomato, and avocado. It was delicious and there was a side of rice and beans, so it was quite filling. After they finished their meals, Jason said, "I suppose you could teleport home if you want to sleep in your own bed."

"No. I'm part of the team here and it feels like I should just stay here with you guys. I only went home to shower to save the water I would use."

"Okay, then, I'm going to read stuff on my phone, and I'll wish you a good night."

Michelle nodded and planned to duplicate his agenda for the evening. After an uneventful night, Michelle felt much better the next day, as did her partners. They were in a holding pattern to find if the city had a drug-production facility. Sheila had two additional agents arriving from Panama and she would split off the team, moving Jason and Michelle to another part of the city.

She considered there to be two missions in Venezuela—one to destroy the drug-production facilities and a second to capture the scientist who created this monster drug. She had one group of analysts focused on buildings and another on scientists.

"The government has taken over the universities in Venezuela. Either they have used the courts to ban any material that says something bad about Chavez or Maduro or they deny the universities funds. Venezuela had an autonomous university system, so first Chavez set up his own university system to compete against the existing schools. Then they started denying those autonomous schools funding. Last year they tried to criminally prosecute a physician in Maracaibo for saying that hospitals didn't have enough masks for staff. That physician now lives in another country.

"In our search for the botanist, the scientist might be a believer in the current government or might be threatened with death or imprisonment if they don't find a plant such as a jimson weed that can be used as a new form of illegal drugs. We won't know the answer to that until we have a chance to question them in the US."

"I assume that all the major Venezuelan cities have universities. Are we in the right city?" Jason asked.

"That's the second piece of news I have for you today. We've had the soil and the plant analyzed, and the growing area based on the composition of the soil is southeast of Lake Maracaibo in the low hills. Our scientists gave us great detail about the dirt which I won't bore you with. We have our satellites looking for both the plants and a greenhouse. Given the poverty in Venezuela, we presume that the plants are started outdoors as that is cheaper than building a massive greenhouse. I assume the Venezuelan botanists get the plants started probably in a large outdoor area, and then at a certain size they are transported to greenhouses attached to the drug-production facility. The geographic area in question has lots of open land and would be suited to a large crop."

"Did your experts say how long the plants take to grow from seed to harvesting?" Michelle asked.

"They germinate after three to four weeks, and then take another six to eight weeks to reach their full size. It's an 'annual,' which means that it blooms during a single growing season. I'm reading you what our experts said. I don't have a green thumb, nor much interest at all in plants, so this may as well have been written in a foreign language for me," Sheila said.

"So are you moving us closer to the University area or out of the city and toward the southeast?" Jason asked.

"We're moving you closer to the University. After the scientist cultivated this plant and strengthened its potency, they wouldn't be needed on a farm to watch it grow every day, or at least that's what our experts say."

"Okay, then, we'll move closer to the University. Should we stay in deserted lodgings or grab a hotel room?"

"Now that we know you have the capacity to get yourself and Jason out of danger, I'm less concerned about the Venezuelan government finding you. That said, as good case officers you should try to live anonymously which means finding a vacant building. If you two are on your own, Michelle can fetch all the food and water you need. Any questions?"

The call ended and they briefly stopped by to thank Antonio and Enrique for working with them. They checked out of the hotel saying that they were flying to Panama City. They had checked and one of the six flights a day landed in Panama City, so it was a reasonable cover. They were worried about running into the two agents in the future as they were in very different parts of the city. They headed away from the registration desk and toward the hallway that contained bathrooms. Once there and after a quick check to make sure no one was looking at them, Michelle wrapped Jason and teleported them to a tree-lined area between two university buildings. It was a dangerous thing to do as she didn't know the flow of people in that area. But school wasn't supposed to be back in session for another month, and the satellite photos had shown few cars in the parking lot.

A millisecond later they both looked around at the trees. Michelle was always quick to do a 360-degree scan when she used her teleportation skill. This time there were no people in their vicinity. They had safely moved from one end of town to nearly fifty blocks away in the blink of an eye. Interestingly enough, they had both worn backpacks and the backpacks arrived with them.

"I don't understand how I can move you from one place to another, let alone for your backpack, but I'm not arguing with the results. This will make our missions so much better and faster as long as we're not partnered with someone else."

"Your skill also makes me safer on our missions. Not only can you fetch food and water to keep us alive, with the simple effort of wrapping yourself around me, you can save me from the direst of circumstances. It's really an amazing talent and I'm glad I kept investigating your disappearances in our prior case. I, of course, will guard your secret with my dying breath. I know that sounds cheesy and melodramatic, but I mean it."

"Actually, you should thank Sheila for having those five-gallon water bottles and then making the connection. It might've taken me a while longer to figure that out. I'm glad you're comfortable with me dragging your body from one spot to another. It's really quite freaky. On that note, let's go find a place to stay."

Besides the great downturn in the economy suffered by Venezuelans, Maracaibo was one of the towns hit the most by the pandemic. Between the economy, death, and disease, large swaths of businesses in the city had been wiped out. Jason and Michelle had their choice of empty buildings they could occupy while the agency searched for the botanist. Michelle gathered supplies to make their stay comfortable, including air mattresses to avoid hard floors, water, warm pizza, and an endless supply of water jugs to flush toilets. She planned to teleport them back to their apartments every third day to get showers and clean clothes before returning to their deserted building.

On the second day there, Michelle asked, "Can you think of anything we can do to help the agency find this botanist?"

"Good question. I wonder if the university has a botanical garden or any other kind of plant display? We could teleport to the southern part of the lake, but it's a big area and that seems like we would be looking for a needle in a haystack."

"How about if we find where botany is taught and explore the building in the middle of the night? Maybe we'll luck out and find the plant inside the building."

"That's a good suggestion. Let's text Sheila and tell her what we're up to. It's not that we need her permission, though I suppose we do since she's our boss. We're just letting her know where to look for our dead bodies."

"That's a pessimistic thought for how our building search might go. I'll text her now and let's go to work and figure out where that building might be on campus."

Sheila was pleased with their idea. The analysts must have been making slow progress identifying where this botanist might be located. She said she would have her people find the building in question.

"That suits me. I figure the fewer electronic transmissions we make, the better," Jason said.

Michelle nodded in agreement and pulled out a deck of cards. They got a call a few hours later.

"We researched social media platforms and thankfully the students post pictures. Not only do we have a few buildings for you to search, but we might also even have a narrow list of botanists. We originally targeted just Zulia University, but now that we looked at social media, we came up with a couple of universities with botany professors. We're sending you over the coordinates of the buildings that might house botany labs."

"Not to tell you what your job is, Sheila, but social media is the first place I would have looked to find the botanist," Michelle said.

"We did look at social media to find the botanist. The trouble was, we were looking only from a teacher perspective and not the student perspective. In this case, the students were a lot more informative than the teachers."

"Ah, I understand. We're going into these buildings after dark and long after when any professor should be at work. If we do find someone with activity near the plants in question, should we just grab them and bring them to Langley? For all I know, we'll grab a student and not the professor."

"Bring whoever you find near the plants. If they turn out to be a botany student, we'll give them the opportunity of continuing their education at an American university. I would think that would be pretty hard to turn down for the average Venezuelan."

"Okay we'll start sending you pictures later tonight," Michelle said. "If I do find someone to teleport, I'll be aiming for your office, so don't put any new furniture in it for me to bump into."

"Good luck," were Sheila's final words before she clicked off.

"What do we do if there are two people in the lab?" Michelle asked.

"You grab the one closest to you, and I'll hold onto the other one until you come back. We're talking about a process that will take less than a minute to move two suspects and then you come back for me," Jason said with a smile.

"Sheila's office is getting crowded, but yes I'll come back for you though I might move you to your apartment and just stay out of the chaos that will be her office. Can you imagine what it will be like to have two Spanish-speaking people unable to explain how they left their Venezuelan town and ended up in the CIA office?"

"Not our problem. We're just trying to put an end to these lethal jimson plants and hope that we prevent them from ever being grown again. Then we'll get a break of a few days to weeks depending on the crisis in the world and we'll be out worrying about a new world problem."

"Maybe the agency will want me to rescue some hostage somewhere. Now that I have a new way of rescuing them, it will go a lot faster."

"That's true. As bad as this drug problem is here in Venezuela, the fact that you discovered something new about your teleportation skill may, in the end, save many more lives than you can imagine."

Michelle nodded and said, "Let's get back to planning our visit to these buildings. I would think that they might have security, but given how expensive that is and the lack of electricity, maybe they won't dink around with alarming university lab buildings. I don't recall taking biology in college. My degree is in criminal justice. How about you?"

"I skipped the biology thing too. My degree is in political science. The funny thing about that degree now, some thirty years since I earned it, is that many countries of the world have changed, and what I learned then no longer applies. I guess I should've done something more practical."

Michelle smiled and they returned their eyes to the images

sent by the agency. The agency suggested the order the buildings be examined based on what they read on social media. That was as good a reason as any to follow their instructions.

"I hope we don't pick up two people in each location. Can you imagine? At the end of the night Sheila could have ten people in her office being offered free American educations!"

"The agency will keep the whole thing quiet, but it would be good entertainment to watch."

"Let's plan on leaving at the stroke of midnight. It's seven o'clock now. Do you want something hot for dinner? Or we could continue playing cards. By the way, I have all black clothing with me and a ski cap as that is standard agency apparel. Do you have the same?" Michelle asked.

"I have the apparel and I'd rather read a book for a while and then play some cards. If I do that in the reverse order, I might fall asleep."

"Ditto."

# CHAPTER 23

Michelle and Jason teleported to the first building they planned to search. They did a quick assessment as to whether any lights were on in the building other than those perhaps needed for hallway safety. There were none. Michelle imagined the picture the agency had sent for this building and soon they were inside. It was four stories and there were a lot of spaces to check. They discussed how they should do a building search. Jason didn't have keys and no skill with lock picking. He would take every door that had glass and peer inside with the flashlight to determine whether there were plants inside. Michelle would teleport inside each closed door to see what was inside. It was slower than they wanted as Jason discovered that he couldn't always see into all the angles in each room. In the first building, they found no people and no plants.

The second building was smaller, but all its doors were wooden and so Jason was of little help. Michelle spent time teleporting to just the other side of the door and then turning her flashlight on. The building took almost as long as the first one even though it was smaller.

They repeated the process of staking out before entering the third building. They could see light from one of the building's rooms, but it wasn't bright overhead light. They decided to start on that floor and check out that room, and they hit pay dirt.

"This is the same plant in the same kind of container that I removed from Ciudad Guayana. It's smaller; the light we saw from the outside must be growing lights. I wonder what we should do now," Michelle asked.

"We should talk to Langley, but I think we want to get a few cameras in here. Maybe that will tell us who the botanist is."

"That's a great idea. Do you have any with you?"

"No. Got any spares at your condominium from the last mission?" Jason asked.

"I think I do. I'm going to teleport you back to our base. Then I'll teleport home and grab the cameras and stick them around this room."

"I think you should take me with you to your condo and then we'll both come back together to plant the cameras and return to base. What if, when we come back here there's someone in this room? Let's teleport outside this building or in the hallway. I think you're worried for nothing," Jason said.

She reluctantly agreed and followed Jason's plan. A very short time later they were placing cameras in the room before she teleported them both back to base.

"What are you so worried about? If someone sees us, we disappear."

"I'm scared I'll screw up and leave you behind. I've been doing this on my own for over five years and my instincts might take over my common sense. Therefore, I'd rather have you safely tucked away so I don't have to worry about making sure I curl correctly around you."

"Okay, I understand. Let's log in and then transmit the camera information to Sheila so her people can watch the cameras. We should get some sleep as it's now nearly four in the morning."

Michelle was exhausted and fell asleep before Jason finished sending the information to Sheila. They spoke with Langley later that day after they had time to watch what was going on in the lab.

"We lucked out. The analysts identified the botanist and her actions. She was touring a government representative through her lab. She said she set up a relationship with the government to get a per plant royalty. They are trying to stiff her for the plants in the factories we blew up and she's not accepting that decision. She also named all the other locations of her factories and asked the representative to increase security. She's exhibit A for 'loose lips sink ships.' We'll be able to show the film at the United Nations to further nail them for their actions, and to get ourselves off the hook for destroying their buildings. Antonio and Enrique and their team have another five factories to destroy. We need you to grab her. However, we first want to follow her movement to see if we can locate her plants grown outside the university. If they have acres of those plants, we need to throw some weed killer on the stuff."

"Does she carry a purse? Ideally, we could put a tracker in there and on her car. Although, it's at least a four-hour car ride to reach the southeast area of the lake. Perhaps she flies or has a high-speed boat. The lake is nearly one-hundred miles long."

"Just a moment. I'll call you back."

They waited a few minutes, and Sheila did call back with the news that she didn't have a purse in the room and the analysts were locating her office. Once they located it, they would let Michelle know so she could teleport inside to drop a tracker after she first picked one up from Sheila's office.

"Really, the best place from which to teleport her is out on her farm. There are fewer people around to watch her disappear," Jason said. "Having seen her, you'll need my help subduing her for transport. We probably need some help from Sheila on this one. Maybe the CIA knows of a drug that would make her cooperative long enough to teleport her, but you don't want her unable to stand on her own two feet. I can't see you teleporting a floppy adult."

"When I grab a supply of trackers and cameras from her office, I'll ask Sheila to have the agency come up with something. I don't want the agency giving me something to inject her with. Maybe we could just tie her up and have the little black plane come for her."

Michelle paused as she read a text from Sheila. She had the electronic equipment in her office ready for pick-up.

"On further thought, we will tie her up and I'll lie on the ground and hug her all the way to Langley. I like that idea. I don't want to be involved with giving people medication sanctioned or not. So yes, I need your help and some long rope to strap her down. Then Sheila will have to deal with her in her office all trussed up and I'm sure screaming in Spanish. Got to fly to Sheila's office."

Jason found the silence disconcerting; one moment his partner was planning their mission and in the next, she was gone like she had never been there. Just as he was thinking about her absence in detail, she reappeared holding a small bag to her chest.

"Okay. I'm on standby to teleport to the botanist's office when I get the call. Wish me luck."

"You don't need luck. You're good at your job."

"Thanks."

There was no call for the remainder of the day. Perhaps their target was teaching students or just rarely walked into the lab. Around midnight Michelle went to the building and then the hallway where the professor's office was located and teleported inside so she would be familiar with the layout. She placed a camera at desk level and returned to Jason.

By the next morning, the call arrived. Her friends in Langley could see the purse sitting on the desk. Michelle grabbed her trackers and teleported into the office but out of camera range. They didn't know about her teleportation skill, and it was best not to let them in on her secret. She dropped the tracker in the woman's purse, and she saw a briefcase on the floor. She dropped a second tracker into one of its zippered compartments and she backed out of camera range and was gone.

She teleported back to their building and Jason.

"Were you interrupted?"

"No, the agency must have called as soon as she walked into the plant room. I'm sure that Sheila told them I was in the hallway and had excellent lock-picking skills. How else could I have gotten there so quickly? I dropped a tracker into her purse and briefcase, so hopefully, she carries one of those items when she visits the crop."

They passed another hour thanks to the books that each of them had on their phones.

Jason was about to say something when Langley called.

"There's a little airport near the university and she seems to be headed toward it. Your thought that she might fly south was accurate. We'll monitor from here and see where it lands. If you look at the southern part of the lake, there are few airports as there are few people. So I think she is going for a dirt road somewhere."

Michelle looked over at Jason and asked, "Do you have the rope? Sheila, are you ready to receive one botanist?"

"Rope?" Sheila asked.

"She's not going to come willingly so I'll tie her up so I can teleport her."

"We have drugs for that."

"No. I have Jason, that's enough."

"Okay, just get her here and find that crop."

"Got it."

The call ended and Michelle and Jason watched the plane travel south along the east side of the lake. The lake was famous for having unique weather patterns given that it was such a large body of water. It made sense that the plane would want to stay over land. It also made sense to cross the lake at its narrowest point which was close to where it took off. Jason had his backpack ready to go with rope and zip ties. Michelle had pepper spray in case another deterrent was needed. Jason also now had his agency-issued gun, but that was only for the direst of circumstances.

The agency hoped to have a still shot of where she landed. The question was, would the plane land next to the jimson crop or would she need a car to get her there? They wondered if she was visiting her plant farm as the Venezuelans needed to restart production of the drug to replace what they lost in the explosions. Maybe a truck was meeting her at the crop, as surely the small plane couldn't carry the number of plants necessary to restart drug manufacturing.

The agency notified them that the plane was slowing its speed and altitude, so it was likely landing. There was no airport in the area, so they would be landing somewhere on a road. The plane landed and rolled to a rest. The tracker left the plane and she apparently got in a car as the tracker picked up speed again. After a twenty-minute drive into the low hills, the car stopped.

The agency sent Michelle a picture of the area and she gave Jason a tight hug and teleported them to a collection of trees close to where the botanist was last tracked. They had eyes on her, and other people were surrounding her listening to her orders, judging by their body language.

Michelle whispered to Jason, "I was hoping she would be here alone. But it makes sense that they would need someone here with the crop. I think I see the jimson weed. I'm going to move closer just to verify it, take a picture to send to the agency, and I'll return."

The moment he nodded she was gone, and just as quickly she returned. She showed him her screen and there was a picture of the jimson plant. They found the crop that needed to be destroyed. Now they just needed to figure out how to take the woman down.

"Do you see any weapons that anyone is carrying?" Jason asked.

"I don't, but their clothing is loose, and they may have guns close by. Maybe we should look at the area around the plane and go after her there with just the pilot to defend her?"

"We could let her go home and get her in her university office, but I know Sheila is expecting you to turn up with her at any moment in her office. Why don't you move around and get a complete count of the number of people here and then we'll discuss our next steps."

Michelle disappeared, moving around the property to get an accurate count of the number of men. Jason watched the work the men were doing, and it was relatively labor-intensive. They were hand-digging out every plant and putting it in a container presumably for shipping. He thought he was hearing another motor vehicle approach. It became louder and then came into view. It was likely as big a truck as could navigate the type of roads that existed here. It looked like it would hold several hundred plants. They would have to make sure that the truck couldn't leave. This whole operation needed to be destroyed.

Michelle reappeared and said, "Besides our botanist, there appear to be seven men digging the plants out of the ground. The truck that's clearly going to be used to ship the plants has a driver and that makes eight. That's too many men for us to take on."

"Do we know if she drove herself here from the plane?"

"I can't imagine she keeps a car parked here for visits to the field. Someone probably picked her up. Do you want to take her and the driver on while they're on the road back to the plane? With your gun, you could shoot out the tires. I'd take a knife to her tires now but I'm afraid that the car wouldn't get out of here."

"Maybe we toss a large rock at the windshield. Except you don't want to hug her if she's full of glass fragments."

"I could jump on the car, which should scare them enough to hit the brakes."

"You would get injured. I'm back to liking rocks. Let's check this road out to see if there's a good spot to launch rocks from. I'd like to put one through the driver's side windshield and then through his side window. That would hopefully keep the glass off of her."

"How about throwing a crowbar through the wheels? If we find some deep divots in the road, they probably have to go very slowly at that point. Maybe we could slide a bar through the wheels during those slow parts."

"Let's ask Langley for suggestions," Jason said. "I don't like any of our ideas so far."

They posed the question and got a good suggestion. Start a fire close by in a couple of places, except this was near the rainforest and it wasn't nearly dry enough to catch fire. Then Langley suggested lighting the buildings on fire and while the workers were distracted, snatch the woman. Michelle scanned the buildings, and they weren't much. Would the men move to put out the fire and leave the woman alone? She didn't think so, but it was worth a try. Thankfully she had a lighter in her backpack, and she approached the back of the first building and tried to get a fire going. Even though the shack was made out of wood, it had rained a lot in this area and it was too saturated to catch fire. Then she had an idea.

# CHAPTER 24

They could light the truck on fire. That would cause great panic and consternation.

"Do you know how to light that truck on fire?" Michelle asked Jason.

"No, but that's a brilliant idea. Can we pull the hood open and put a lighted object in the engine compartment? Maybe we should light the cab on fire? Let's make sure there isn't a fire extinguisher."

They didn't see one, so this seemed like a sound idea. Michelle sacrificed a cotton tank top and soaked it in the gas canister on the back of the truck. *It must need extra gas to get this far*, she thought. She then lit it and threw it in the open cab window. *Thank you, driver, for your help, she thought.* The open window would mean plenty of oxygen for the fire to burn. It helped that there were tears in the seat as that facilitated the fire. They stood back and watched the fire begin to roar; the men noticed, dropped their stuff and ran toward the cab. The woman stayed well back. Her fear of the fire worked perfectly into their plan. Michelle dragged the woman back into the brush as Jason stuffed a dirty t-shirt of his that he had worn the last few days and zip-tied her legs together. He had her hog-tied quickly and Michelle gave the woman the hug of her life and soon found herself lying on the carpet in Sheila's office.

"She's all yours," Michelle said, letting the woman go and standing up. "I'm going to get Jason."

A moment later she was back in the brush where she had left Jason. She didn't immediately see him. She searched for him and found him being held by two men wielding machete knives. She pulled out her pepper spray and hit both of them before quickly giving Jason a tight hug; the next thing she knew, she was shivering in the kitchen of Jason's unheated apartment.

"Oh my gosh, that was close," Michelle said.

"Actually, I've been in tighter circumstances. Before you pepper-sprayed them, we were having a conversation."

"Yeah, right. I saw the beers in your hands and the television channel on a baseball game."

"Okay, we weren't close friends like that, but we would have worked things out."

"Do you want me to return you so you can finish your conversation—perhaps explain why you set their truck on fire and where the woman disappeared to?"

"No, we were almost done. I'm sure they have bigger problems to worry about, like the approach of a crop-dusting plane."

"You really saw a crop-dusting plane?"

"No, but I heard one. It has a very distinct engine sound. We should ask the analysts if the crop is being destroyed. They sure didn't give us much time to get out of the way."

That stopped Michelle in her tracks, and she used her cell phone to call and ask.

Jason was right about the crop duster. It arrived from Colombia and dropped a lethal weed killer on the crop. The weed killer was flammable, and the plane would return after dark and light the field on fire. The agency was trying to make it very hard for Venezuela to restart its illegal drug manufacturing. Having a complete absence of plants would halt their progress for a few years.

Jason and Michelle had to stay away from the agency's head-quarters until the next day so it would look like they flew home. Sheila would brief them tomorrow on the botanist and whatever else they needed to know to close this assignment.

"Alrighty then, I'm going to go home and get cleaned up and sit down with a nice California wine and chill."

"Ah, why don't we go out to a restaurant and celebrate our success at stopping a new and awful drug from reaching American shores?"

"You mean like choose food from a menu that is served hot? Sit on a soft chair in clean clothes with clean skin and hair? I feel like I've been covered in dirt for weeks, and I probably have. I'll accept your invite. See you at seven?"

Both of their phones rang simultaneously with a text message. They both took a moment to read, and Michelle groaned.

"I'm starting to feel like the agency has a thousand urgent fires to put out and I'm their favorite firefighter even though I know nothing about hoses and water."

Jason laughed at her description and said, "It's the sign of a job well done. At least this next case appears to take place in the United States, so we'll have water, food, and a soft bed hopefully."

"True, and it does sound like an assignment after my own heart. I'll let you respond to Sheila that we'll see her in the morn-ing. At least she's giving us a few days between cases. I just want to enjoy tonight and not be looking over my shoulder for the bad guys to be on my tail."

The next day they were in Sheila's office for a debrief. Sheila started with the Botanist.

"Her name is Professor Angela Fernandez and we made a deal with her. She'll spend years in a comfortable federal prison. After that, she'll wear a tracker for five years. In turn, she gave us the details of her plan to get rich from the jimson weed. We recorded her conversation and the fact that they were testing the drug on their own citizens just to assure themselves that it was addictive and lethal. Her testimony has been sent to The Hague for the International Court of Justice to charge Venezuela's leaders involved with the plan."

"How about the existing facilities? Have Antonio and Enrique destroyed those sites?" Michelle asked.

"Yes, and we gave them some help so all five remaining factories have been reduced to rubble. We asked Ms. Fernandez if we had all the locations, and she looked at our list and said we did. I hope that's true. We went back to the truck you lit on fire to see if it had a record of where it made deliveries, but we couldn't find anything."

"How about the private plane that took Ms. Fernandez to the field? Is there record of it flying to other locations?" Jason asked.

"We haven't tracked it down yet, but our analysts say it is unlikely that they delivered plants via plane as most small planes make the most money running other illicit drugs, rather than delivering plants. We have our fingers crossed that Ms. Fernandez was telling the truth. She's very motivated by money. She was quick to provide details so that other people in Venezuela couldn't make money on the operation she developed," Sheila said.

"How will you know if someone else creates this plant? Did she leave notes behind on how she created the plant? I thought you said it was genetically enhanced, and so another botanist could follow her instructions," Michelle said.

"It seems that everyone in Venezuela is paranoid about how the government will get its greedy hands into their business. Ms. Fernandez kept no notes on the creation of her plant for fear the government would take the notes from her, and stop her royalty stream. That's a piece of good news for us. Now. . . . onto your next assignment."

## The End

# ABOUT THE AUTHOR

I reside in Northern California with my rescue dog and cat. I love to travel, play sports, read, and drink wine and beer. I enjoy the diversity of the world and I'm always watching people and events for story ideas. All of my stories are generated by my imagination, I don't use AI to write books.

If you would like to sign up for my bi-weekly blog and announcement of new books, please follow this link: https://www.AlecPecheBooks.com

While you're waiting for the next story, if you would be so kind as to leave a review for this book, that would be great. I appreciate all the feedback and support. Reviews buoy my spirits and stoke the fires of creativity.

Readers that sign up for my blog receive a free prequel novelette for the Jill Quint Series.

# ALSO BY ALEC PECHE

**Jill Quint, MD Forensic Pathologist Series**

Time's Up (prequel short story)

Vials

Chocolate Diamonds

A Breck Death

Death On A Green

A Taxing Death

Murder At The Podium

Castle Killing

Crescent City Murder

Sicilian Murder

Opus Murder

Forensic Murder

Return to the Scene of the Crime (short story)

Embers of Murder

Ashes to Murder

Mint Death

**Damian Green Series**

Red Rock Island

Willow Glen Heist

The Girl From Diana Park

Evergreen Valley Murder

Long Delayed Justice

**Michelle Watson Series**

Now You Don't See Me

Where Did She Go?

How Did She Get There?

**<u>Dog Humor</u>**

Eat, Play, Poop: Letters to my parents from camp

**<u>New Urban Fantasy Series - Stephanie Jones</u>**

The Awakening at Lake Tahoe (short story)

Witch's Medicine (2024)